Lady Maclairn, The Victim Of Villany

A Novel
Vol. III

by
Mrs. Hunter

Lady Maclairn, The Victim Of Villany
A Novel
Vol. III
by Mrs. Hunter

Copyright © 2024

All Rights reserved.

No part of this publication may be reproduced, stored in a retrieval system, or transmitted in any form or by any means, electronic, mechanical, photocopying or Otherwise, without the written permission of the publisher.
The author/editor asserts the moral right to be identified as the author/editor of this work.

ISBN: 978-93-62761-07-1

Published by

DOUBLE 9 BOOKS

2/13-B, Ansari Road
Daryaganj, New Delhi – 110002
info@double9books.com
www.double9books.com
Tel. 011-40042856

This book is under public domain

ABOUT THE AUTHOR

Mrs. Hunter, a prominent author of the Victorian era, showcases her literary prowess in her masterpiece, "Lady Maclairn, the Victim of Villainy: A Novel." With meticulous attention to detail and a keen understanding of human nature, Mrs. Hunter skillfully crafts a narrative that captivates readers from the very first page. Set against the backdrop of nineteenth-century England, the novel delves into the complexities of society, shedding light on the intricacies of class, morality, and deception. Through the protagonist, Lady Maclairn, Mrs. Hunter explores themes of innocence, betrayal, and the consequences of societal expectations. As the plot unfolds, readers are drawn into a world of suspense and intrigue, where secrets lurk behind every polite facade. Mrs. Hunter's vivid descriptions and nuanced characterizations breathe life into the story, transporting readers to a bygone era filled with romance and scandal. "Lady Maclairn, the Victim of Villainy" stands as a testament to Mrs. Hunter's literary talent and her ability to craft a compelling narrative that resonates with readers across generations. With its blend of mystery, drama, and romance, this novel continues to enthrall audiences, cementing Mrs. Hunter's place among the great authors of Victorian literature.

CONTENTS

CHAPTER I 7
CHAPTER II 14
CHAPTER III 22

CHAPTER I

Again must the reader be contented with my pen, in order to supply the interrupted course of Miss Cowley's letters.

From the period already described the lovers were left to their own discretion, and the direction of Counsellor Steadman; who, availing himself of Mr. Sinclair's information, decidedly supported them in their attachment; and, in the words of the fond father, "became a teacher of doctrines, which had silenced his authority, if they had not convinced his conscience." As this was said with an acquiescent smile, it was understood. Besides this no other consequence resulted from Mr. Sinclair's letter, as Miss Cowley gave her lover to understand, that she meant not to marry till Mr. Flamall's power had ceased. She urged this point with her usual disinterested spirit. "I will be mistress of myself and my fortune," said she, "and manifest to the world my own judgment, in selecting a man worthy of both. I can be as proud as Mr. Hardcastle, and I can have my scruples: my husband shall not lose an ample inheritance, because a girl is impatient to bear his name. We shall be happy; in the mean time, you my Horace are engaged in the sacred duties of friendship: persevere, and rest assured of Rachel Cowley's faith and love."

It is to be regretted, that, from motives of delicacy, Mr. Hardcastle's letters are not permitted to appear; and I cannot but lament that so fair an opportunity escapes me of confuting an opinion, so boldly and erroneously asserted, that "a man in love must write like a fool." Had no impediment been opposed to my wishes, I could have produced incontestible proofs, that love and nonsense have no natural affinity. Horace Hardcastle's understanding was neither enslaved by beauty, nor the dupe of a youthful inclination; nor was Miss Cowley the child of vanity. Rhapsody and flattery were equally useless to their rational views and virtuous attachment. The hopes of meriting each other's esteem imparted to their language the simplicity of truth and the unstudied graces of nature. The tribute of Horace's admiration was directed to the cultivating the taste and forming the judgment of the woman he loved; and Miss Cowley, with a well-grounded confidence in his *principles*, as well as in his superior advantages in learning, assiduously profited from the lessons of a guide too honest to betray, and too quick-sighted to be betrayed.

Rational love-letters, in a novel, might, perhaps, with some sort of readers, have been deemed an equivalent for the absence of the marvellous; and sensible as I am and must be of the deficiency of my work in this respect, I have urged my request with persevering importunity, although without success. To my plea, that Mr. Hardcastle's letters would, at least, give *novelty* to my *novel*, I am told, that a lover with his eyes open would be the disgrace of a circulating library, and the utter ruin of the writer's fame as a novelist; and in reply to the obvious defect of a work stripped of its essential support, I am advised humbly to request my young female readers, to supply this deficiency by reading their own billet-doux, which, I am assured, will give all the interest to the work so anxiously desired. "Be contented with the title of a faithful historian, though perhaps to some, a dull story teller," added Mr. Hardcastle. "You have, in my opinion, said enough of your heroine to convince your readers that she could not love a fool or a coxcomb. Leave me to the enjoyment of this conviction. I am as little qualified for the hero of a popular novel, as you are for writing a fashionable one. With the materials before you, you may produce an offering to common sense; but my letters would neither lull to sleep a craving imagination, nor excite the sensibility of any 'Miss Lydia Languish.' They were dictated by truth and sincerity, and addressed to a reasonable being. My glory is confined to one conclusion; and the conqueror of worlds is unenvied! Horace Hardcastle was beloved by a virtuous woman; and that woman was Rachel Cowley! Surely this will satisfy your readers! If it does not, I pity them; nor can your honest heart reform them." I gave up the contest; for his manly face glowed with conscious worth, and contented ambition. Having again found the thread of my narrative, I once more re-assume my pleasing task.

LETTER XXXII

From Miss Cowley to Miss Hardcastle.

Letters are arrived, my dear Lucy, from our island. Fortunately, I was at the Abbey when they were read at the hall. I rejoice that it so happened, for I am yet but a novice in counterfeiting; and you will judge that the contents of these letters required on my part a complete command of my features. On returning home to supper I found the Baronet alone, and his air more disturbed than I liked. "I am glad you are returned," said he, with eagerness. "We have been very much surprised to-day; and Miss Flint is seriously indisposed by the intelligence we have had from Jamaica." The history of the secret marriage followed. "Lady Maclairn," continued he, "entreats you will excuse her appearing to-night. She is much displeased with her son's conduct in the course of this business. She thinks he has been deficient on the point of honour with you. He ought to have proclaimed his engagement the moment he heard of Mr. Cowley's intentions in his favour." — "He acted from an opinion much more delicate," replied I, "for he gave me credit for sentiments corresponding with his own, and he judged perfectly right in leaving to Mr. Flamall a business of his own forging, and in which we had nothing to do. But," continued I, "from your statement of this affair as it relates to Mr. Philip Flint, there appears but little for regret. His brother approves of his choice you say?" — "Yes," replied the Baronet, "he speaks warmly in praise of the lady; and the romance is likely to finish better than most of those in which Cupid is prime minister. Even his mother would be satisfied with the *denouement* were she left to herself; but Mr. Flamall is offended, and we dare not be placable." Sir Murdoch coloured. I smiled, and observed that he would be polite, and bend to the rising fortune of his nephew. "You do not yet know him," answered he with agitation. "Indeed I do," answered I with gaiety, "and had I known his nephew, we would have effectually cured him of match-making by our joint labours. I am only angry that I have had so little share in his present defeat." The conversation next turned on Miss Flint's vexation and grief, of which we both erroneously judged as it will appear hereafter.

In the morning, the incomprehensible Lady Maclairn appeared with a face as pale as death, and with solemnity of manner, though with great composure, she thus addressed me. "It is with much satisfaction, my dear Miss Cowley, that I am able to recall to my memory my perfect submission to your request and Sir Murdoch's wishes. I have not importuned you on the subject of my son's pretensions. I rejoiced at the prohibition, which pleased me as much as yourself. I was not a stranger to my brother's ambitious and sanguine prospects for his nephew; but it was not so clear to me that Philip would always remain docile to his projects. The late event has convinced me that I judged rightly. And all I have now to wish is, that my son's mode of effecting his happiness may turn out better than the schemes of his uncle." "Never doubt it, madam," said I eagerly; "at any rate he will be happy for a season, and that is more than his uncle could make him. But what says Miss Flint to this love match?" "She has shown her affection on this occasion," replied her Ladyship. "My brother, by his violent invectives, has raised an antagonist where he expected an auxiliary. She is more offended by Mr. Flamall's resentment than by her brother's imprudence, and only laments his not having confided to her the secret of his heart. She foresees that Oliver Flint's kindness and generosity will give him claims unfriendly to her wishes; and she deplores the loss of her favourite, as fatal to her hopes. I have, as usual, suppressed my feelings on this subject. I was never judged competent to the concerns of this child's establishment in the world. I bless God that he has escaped the pernicious consequences of being made of too much importance. If he be happy, I shall be satisfied." She drew her son's letter from her pocket: it was like most of those which are written on such occasions. The old man's pleased me better; it is addressed to Miss Flint, and exhibits a cheerful mind and a benevolent heart. He begs her good offices to reconcile Lady Maclairn's to the marriage, and adds that Philip, by his timidity and secrecy, had lost one child which might have been saved, and with him, that was his greatest fault; for that he had got a wife who pleased him, and every other friend, except Mr. Flamall; "but I shall take care," adds he, "to settle that gentleman's future controul over my children. You would be as fond of the little wife as we are, my dear Lucretia," continues the good man, "if you knew her; she is a pretty, amiable creature, and has won my heart already. I trust I shall live to share the happiness to which I have been useful. Philip is a worthy lad, and he is my peculiar care: have no fears for him, for he is able to walk alone, we want no *tutors*. So you may tell Mr. Flamall, if you please: and Philip's mother may rest satisfied that his conduct is such as reflects no dishonour on his character. I could say more, but it is needless. We are all happy at present, thanks to Providence!"

I observed that Mr. Oliver Flint's letter was a satisfactory one. "Certainly," replied she, "as far as it goes; but there is yet secrecy in the business, and with me concealment portends danger." She was summoned to Miss Flint, who is still much indisposed. I am going to ramble with the Baronet.

(In continuation.)

—Last night after supper Lady Maclairn again brought forward her son's marriage, "I could have wished," said she, turning to me, "that Philip had been more explicit in regard to his engagements with his uncle. I cannot but think he was very wrong in permitting my brother, for an instant, to entertain the hopes he did; and however these hopes stood removed from every chance of succeeding, yet I am certain that Mr. Flamall will be painfully affected by a concealment, which he will judge an indelible disgrace on Philip's honour. He certainly ought to have prevented his uncle's entertaining the prospects he has done." "I will have no judgment passed on *my lover*," replied I, with unaffected gaiety; "all stratagems are lawful under unusurped power; and till I can discover a better reason for my censure than his keeping his own secrets, I shall esteem Mr. Philip Flint." "I have, however, often reflected," said Sir Murdoch, "that in these secret engagements, there is one danger which is rarely insisted on. We can expatiate on the evils of what are justly called imprudent marriages, and inconsiderate connexions; but we seldom think of the deviations from the road of truth which they necessarily force the unwary to tread. The plots and contrivances, the duplicity and deceit, which ordinarily enter into a youthful intrigue, are in my opinion more serious evils, than the difficulties so commonly annexed to a *love match*, as such clandestine engagements are called. The native innocence and rectitude of the mind is broken into; deceit is become familiar, and has been found useful to the purpose of the passions; and it ought not to surprise any one, that a young man, or a young woman, who has attained the desired object by the road of contrivance and imposition, should continue to profit by their acquaintance with them, whenever it suits their views or inclinations."

Never shall I forget the countenance of Lady Maclairn! She had her eyes fixed, and her brows elevated; her breath was short, and her colour forsook her, but as it appeared in spots on her bosom. God knows whether I judged right, but I hesitated not a moment. I rose abruptly, and brushing her neck with my hand, I said, "It is not a spider." She made no reply, but drank some water from the glass before her. Malcolm, praising my courage, and gently reproving his mother's dread of so harmless an insect, insisted on her drinking some wine. She complied, and in a tone of ill-affected gaiety drank to her *deliverer*: and I am persuaded, Lucy, that for the moment *I was her deliverer*. Mrs. Allen observed her extreme distress as well as myself, and our reasonings are endless. We know not the heart of Lady Maclairn! Receive the affectionate farewell of mine which you do know, in all its weaknesses and wanderings.

Rachel Cowley.

LETTER XXXIII

From Miss Cowley to Miss Hardcastle.

So so! Ethusiasm has her votaries, I find, even at Heathcot! Let me see: you say in your last, "my father entirely agrees with you, my dear Rachel, that Miss Howard is nor an object for the libertine's rude gaze, nor for the assaults of an unfeeling world." "You have not been more generous than discriminating, &c." Mr. Sedley, too; well, what does Mr. Sedley think of this girl? Why, that "the casket is worthy of the pure gem it incloses;" and then comes the *sober* praise of Lucy Hardcastle, "Mary Howard is nature's master-piece." I am satisfied, and leave you to decide on my talents for hyperbole. Did I not tell you that I was describing *something* more worthy of my pen than beauty?—but I will spare you.

I suppose Eliza, sends you the parish news. Has she informed Mary of the direful effects which the death of Mrs. Snughead, and the recent advice of the good health and expected arrival of her son and heir have produced on her *inconsolable* husband? In spite of his *strait lacings* the gout found its way to his stomach, and he has had a very narrow escape. He has been advised to go to Bath; and we have got a curate, who will correct me in my late idle habit of breaking the Sabbath; for he is, I am told, a very ingenious and worthy young man.

Mrs. Warner in a walk with Mrs. Allen has unburdened her mind, and in her own words "she is out of all patience" to see her lady making herself miserable *for nothing*. "Her spirits were low enough before, for she had been well humbled, about Miss Mary," continued Warner, "and now she is quite broken hearted, poor soul! This marriage, Mrs. Allen, will be the first nail in my poor lady's coffin." "Why should you think so?" observed Mrs. Allen. "His brother is pleased with the lady he has chosen, and all will be well." "This is what I tell her, Madam," replied the honest woman, "and besides that, I have ventured to say, that Mr. Flamall will not dare to tutor the young gentleman, now he is married and master of himself, as one may say, as he did here, and my lady acknowledged that was a comfort to her, although she could not see him. There is the rub, Madam; she doats upon this young man, and between ourselves it is a great pity; for notwithstanding he is a very fine looking young gentleman, and a sweet tempered one to boot, yet there are, as I say, those as good, who want her money more than he does; for she tells me, he will have every shilling of Mr. Oliver's fortune, and that he has already given him a fine plantation, and I know not how many poor negroes. A good deed for them, poor souls! for Mr. Philip is a tender-hearted man." "It was, however, wrong to enter into an engagement of this sort, without consulting his friends," observed Mrs. Allen; "and still worse, not to confess his marriage before he quitted his family." "To be sure it was," answered she, "but if you knew the temper of his uncle, it would not surprise you. He contrived to be master here, though every one feared and hated him." "Not Miss Flint," said Mrs. Allen, smiling: "I have been told he was a favourite with her." "So have I an hundred times," replied Warner; "but her love was worn out, before I came to the hall, and that is nine years ago. No, no: it was always clear to me how he managed to keep his footing here. Whenever any dispute arose, and there was no lack of them, he used to threaten to take away Philip from the hall and carry him to America or France; and my Lady knowing he could do as he pleased with his poor dejected sister, was always afraid that he would take from her this darling and comfort of her life. I am no fool, Madam; and I can assure you that the world has been much mistaken in regard to Miss Flint's liking Mr. Flamall. She loves nothing, nor any one on earth but her brother Philip. This very morning she cried as though her heart was breaking; and said, all was lost to her. 'Why, my dear Madam,' said I, 'you grieve more than his mother does; she hopes to see him again, and why should you despair?' She shook her head and said, 'you know not, Warner, what I suffer.' Poor soul! I do know; but her fretting will never cure her grievance; and after all; you will acknowledge, Madam, that her complaint does not shorten life. To be sure, the unlucky blow she received when getting to her room, in the confusion which followed Miss Howard's fainting, has not mended matters; but time and patience may; and if she would be governed by me, and leave off that pernicious rum and water, she might get better; but between ourselves she yields more and more to the habit, and that only inflames the wound, and she suffers what would kill a horse." "She is happy at least in having so faithful a domestic as yourself near her," observed Mrs. Allen. "I believe she thinks so," answered the good creature, "for although she is an odd woman, and commonly thought a very bad tempered one, I have found her generous to me. She has been a disappointed woman too that is certain; but I soon discovered that she knew who did their duty; and as I faithfully performed mine in the hope of being approved by a master, who knows no distinctions with his servants. I have neither feared her nor flattered her; my character will always support me; for I never lived but at the hall and with one other family, where I am sure of favour whenever I ask it. Sixteen years spent with lady Grenville will get me a place any hour of the day, though she is in her grave." Warner yielded to her gratitude and affection, and the conversation, finished with the character of this lady. Adieu my friend! my sister! judge of my affection by that which thou cherishest for thy

RACHEL COWLEY.

CHAPTER II

LETTER XXXIV
From the same to the same.

Believe me, my dear friend, the slight indisposition which that Chit Alien has magnified into a dangerous fever, was shorter in duration than the alarm she so incautiously produced at Heathcot. It is true that, in order to please Lady Maclairn and to satisfy my nurse, I submitted to the penance of keeping my bed for two days and have for some days since, been pent up in my own apartment. It does youth and vigour no harm, to have from time to time such gentle lessons as the one I have been taught, of the fallacy and fragility of life; but with the cordials of kindness and attention which I have received, the only remaining doubt is whether I shall think of it to any purpose. Sir Murdoch, my first physician at present, or rather my only one, is accused of being like too many of his medical brethren, unwilling to pronounce the patient well, from his relish of his fee. But this is pure malice; and a scandal fabricated by Mrs. Heartley, out of revenge; because he preferred sharing with me a new book, to dining with her; alleging also, that as she had allured my nurse from her charge, it behoved him to watch me. You will do wisely, my dear Lucy, to consider the danger of this tremendous fever, during which Mrs. Allen leaves me to amuse herself. But these romantic girls! they so dearly love the pathetic, that they are never to be trusted with a plain tale. Now I, being a mere matter of fact correspondent; and who, in two lines, had I been permitted, would have told you that I had got a severe cold; now as frankly avow, that I have had a fever-fit, to the full as *pathetic* as any which Allen's imagination pictured to you. But as it happens to be one of that sort which is contagious, I beg you to be prepared for a quick pulse, and an aching head, on perusing the enclosed narration. I have paid the tribute; and have calmed my spirits, by writing to my Horace. Adieu, *pour le présent.*

(In Continuation)

When Mrs. Allen left me, for her walk and her day's holiday, Sir Murdoch took his seat opposite to me. I was making some artificial flowers for Lady Maclairn's vases. The baronet was amused by seeing me, as he said "rival Flora;" and we chatted some little time over the work. At length his silence to a question of mine diverted my attention from my employment, and looking at him, I found he was fallen into one of his absent fits, and as usual, had his eyes fixed on me, with that expression of sadness so peculiarly touching. "Come, my good friend," said I with cheerfulness, "do not suppose I shall permit you to be idle; either take up the book, or wind this skain of silk for me." He smiled and took the silk. "Take heed you do not entangle it," said I, assisting for a moment in the operation, "it is wofully ruffled." "It resembles more closely," replied he calmly, and proceeding cautiously in his task, "the web of my thoughts which you interrupted." But I had found the clue, that had made all smooth within, and with patience I shall succeed in *this* business.

"I was thinking, my dear Miss Cowley," continued he, "when you called me to order, of those means which Providence employs for its gracious purposes of mercy and deliverance, to beings like ourselves, who in the imperfect state in which we are placed, with all the reason of which so many boast, neither can provide for our own good, nor prevent a future evil: I was tracing the chain of events which in their consequences were appointed to heal my wounded mind, and with these considerations, entered the sense of my own short-sightedness, and opposition to the intended remedy; my repugnance to Mr. Flamall's offers of placing you here; the dread of seeing you; and the painful struggles I had in conquering my aversion to the journey to town. As these circumstances arose to my memory, I experienced the truth and vexation they had caused me; and I doubt not my countenance indicated to you that I was disturbed. But what will you think when I tell you, that the first view of you was to me accompanied with an anguish of soul unutterable, and which it makes me faint even to think of? Yet, my dear Miss Cowley, you were the angel of mercy sent to heal me, you spoke, you smiled, I heard your voice, the storm of conflicting sorrows was hushed, my soul was entranced in bliss; for I imagined that I saw before me my sainted Matilda. This lady was my early love, my affianced wife, the pride, the glory of my race! the object with which my life, my honour, and my affection were inseparably connected! Listen to me," added he with solemnity, observing that I was disturbed, "your influence over me has not been effected by your attractive beauty: neither your understanding, your native cheerfulness, nor your tender compassion, would have reached my torpid heart and extinguished sensations. It was your resemblance to his portrait, Miss Cowley, that burst asunder the chains which had weighed me down, and that spoke peace to my harassed spirit." He drew from his bosom the miniature picture of a young lady; and presenting it to me added, that his wife had been surprised by my striking likeness to it. The painting was enamelled and highly finished; and the face was, to speak frankly, lovely. "I am disqualified for a judge," said I, examining it; "were it less beautiful, I might allow my vanity indulgence, and honestly confess, that, I think it does resemble a miniature of me, drawn when last I was in London, for a friend; but this lady was a much fairer woman than I am." "Not as she appeared when I knew her," answered he, replacing the picture; "health and exercise had given such tints to her complexion as no colours I could employ were able to reach. How many times have I had reason to regret the attainment which gave to my aching eyes this faint memorial of her charms! Every time I surveyed this picture was a moment placed to the account of misery, till I saw you: but now it is my consolation to compare its features with yours. I know what you think, but in pity to my infirmity suffer me to enjoy the delusion, which lulls me to repose. You have no parents living. Let me call you *daughter*. Such, had heaven permitted our union, would have been Matilda's child; such, the image of herself, might she have bequeathed me, had"—He could not proceed; but bursting into tears he covered his face. "Call me by any title that pleases you," said I; "none that you will give me can express more reverence and esteem than I have for you. But to render your daughter happy, you must be less susceptible to impressions so unfriendly to your health and comforts." "They have ceased to be afflictive," answered he; "for I can now say with Job, 'My sorrows came in upon me as a wide breaking in of waters; in the desolation they rolled themselves upon me; but my deliverer was at my right hand to save me.' His arm of mercy has been stretched out for me also, and 'I will praise him whilst I have my being.' But let me tell *my child* her *father's* story," added he pensively smiling.—"Another time," replied I, "will be better for us both." "Do you think so?" answered he with a sigh, "then it shall be so; but I should like you to know the man before you, and whom you permit to call you *daughter*. It would relieve my mind to give you a portion of its burden." I could not refuse this appeal, and he proceeded.

HISTORY OF THE MACLAIRN FAMILY

"My father," said Sir Murdoch, "was one of those men who could not abandon their unfortunate monarch in the year 1715, and he was one also of that faithful band who saw their own ruin in the fall of the Stuart line.

"He fled to France, after every hope was lost, and there he entered into a regiment chiefly composed of men like himself, and whose loyalty and courage have well recompensed the country which then sheltered and fed them. With the rank of captain, and an unsullied name, he soon after married a young lady, whose fortune was similar to his own. Her father was major in the same corps; but unable to bear the reverse of fortune, or borne down by the fatigues he had encountered in the royal cause, he died, and left his daughter to a Maclairn"—Sir Murdoch rose, and paced the room—"I was the only fruit of this marriage," resumed he; "my mother I do not remember, for I was only three years old when my father lost this prop of his earthly comforts; but he taught me to revere her name.

"During the contest for dominion, to which I have already alluded, my uncle, Sir Alexander Maclairn, had with more prudence than *honour*, according to the opinion of the adherents to the unhappy Charles, remained for a time inactive, and at length declared himself openly the friend of the established government; but neither his zeal nor his services were further recompensed than by leaving him to the peaceable enjoyment of the wreck of the once prosperous fortune of his ancestors; namely, a castle falling to decay, and the remnant of the estate burdened with a heavy mortgage.

"Time had given stability to the British monarch; and my uncle, desirous of seeing a brother whom he loved and secretly reverenced, employed such means as were necessary to restore my father to his native rocks with security. This intelligence was communicated to him, when I had just reached my nineteenth year, and Sir Alexander, with every argument that affection could suggest, finished his intreaties by reminding my father of his age and infirmities; and the duty they were mutually bound to perform before death closed their eyes. 'All that remains of our name,' added he, 'is in our children. My Matilda shall never lose the title of Maclairn; from her cradle she has been taught to love her cousin, and to your Murdoch do I look for a renovation of that race which it is your duty to perpetuate. Remember that these children are the last hope of an ancient and honourable house, which even in the obscurity of a sunken fortune will retain its place in the annals of true glory; for its sons were brave and its daughters virtuous.' He blessed Providence for its interposition, which had opened his eyes to the folly and madness which the prince's adherents had fallen into, in their attempts to reinstate the proscribed Stuarts; 'and I now bless heaven,' added he, 'that by my moderation I have preserved an asylum for you and a home for our children.'

"My father, disgusted with a foreign service, and languishing to behold his native country, eagerly embraced my uncle's offers. He had long before this event determined that my path in life should not be that of a soldier, and he had with extreme caution repressed in me his own military spirit. I was educated by a Scotchman who had once been a minister of that Master whose religion is *peace*; my leisure hours were filled up by studies of retired ease and tranquillity; and painting and music were familiar to me.

"We were received by my uncle with unaffected joy; and welcomed by a few faithful adherents to our family with those genuine demonstrations of good will and attachment so congenial to the noble and uncorrupted Highlanders. On beholding my cousin Matilda, I blushed as deeply from the consciousness of what had passed in my mind in relation to her, as from surprise on beholding this 'rustic' cousin embellished with all the graces of youth, beauty, and artless manners; and when with ingenuous simplicity she offered me her glowing cheek, her eyes beaming with joy and kindness, I felt that I was unworthy of her goodness. A few months were given to the domestic comforts of my uncle and father, and apparently for the purpose of rivetting my chains. My assiduities met with no check; and *our children* was the common epithet my uncle employed in speaking of us. A more explicit avowal of his wishes followed; and in this conversation Sir Alexander candidly acknowledged that he was under pecuniary difficulties, and unable to establish me in life without some exertions on my part. My father, without knowing the pressure of his brother's difficulties in their full extent, not only saw the expediency, but the utility of my being employed, and he sent me to Aberdeen to study the civil law. During a year, which was thus passed without profit to me but as it led me to a further knowledge of the mathematics, my uncle had gained on my father to listen to his darling project as well as my own; and being offered for me an ensigncy in a regiment destined for Minorca, he gained his point, and I escaped from a pursuit I detested, that of the law. An additional debt was cheerfully incurred on the Maclairn's impoverished acres. My separation from Matilda was softened to me by her father's last words: 'Have ever before you this recompense,' said he, placing at the same time Matilda's hand in mine; 'she will be always a *Maclairn*. Do you so conduct yourself as to return to us worthy of the name.' You will imagine, that my martial spirit was sunk when I received her embrace, and my poor father's blessing: I will not be tedious. During my three years' station at Minorca, I rose to the rank of lieutenant, and lost my father. From that period the cloud of adversity became more portentous. I was frustrated in my expectations of returning home, and receiving the reward I had so arduously strove to merit. But my uncle's ambition had been roused by the partiality of my friends, and he contrived to promote me at the expence of my happiness. I exchanged my post and regiment for one at Gibraltar, in which I ranked as captain. This disappointment of my hopes deeply affected my spirits, and Matilda had apparently shared with me in this trial of our patience. Her letters were more tender than cheerful, and she commonly finished by reminding me of her determined faith and unutterable affection. Gracious God! my trust in thy power was not more solid than my faith in Matilda's truth!

"In the last letter she wrote me, and which is engraven on my memory, she finished *thus:*—'It soothes my depressed spirits, to call thee my wedded lord, and to sign myself thy wife. Are we not one, my Maclairn, in the sight of that Being who has witnessed our vows of truth, of honourable love? Are we not one, though seas and lands part us? Yes, and though worlds should interpose to divide us, we shall meet and be united as kindred spirits, as *one*, in the blessed state of perfect happiness, of permanent felicity. There at least will thy Matilda meet thee, and there will her Maclairn be comforted for his present disappointments.'

"Alas! Miss Cowley, the cloud had burst on my devoted head at the very moment I was unconsciously weeping over this letter, as the precious proof of my security; though it was also as painful a proof of the state of Matilda's spirits. The indolence and pusillanimity of Sir Alexander Maclairn had always been leading traits in his character; these, with other circumstances, had placed him in the power of *a man*, who hated him, merely because his grandfather had served Sir Alexander's in a menial station. Industry had made this man's successors wealthy; and my uncle had, in his difficulties, applied to their more fortunate heir than himself, for money so repeatedly, that he was little more than the ostensible proprietor of his inheritance. His wary and greedy creditor had changed his tone; and frequent hints of the necessity of foreclosing the mortgage, unless my uncle could be more punctual in paying his stipulated interest, were, from time to time, thrown out with increasing seriousness and harshness. In a dilemma of this kind, the laird of Maclairn Castle received a visit from his importunate neighbour, who introduced with much ceremony his only child, a young man, who had lived chiefly in the South with a rich tradesman, his uncle. Hospitality, as much as policy, induced my uncle to welcome the stranger; and the young man repeated his visit. The sight of my beauteous Matilda effected more; he became enamoured, and made his father his confidant. Secure of the estate, he now aspired to the daughter of *a Maclairn*, and without loss of time he proposed an alliance, which at once, as he observed, would settle all accounts between himself and Sir Alexander; his son not desiring a shilling with his daughter; and he added, that he would cancel every mortgage and bond on the day of their marriage. The weak old man listened to this infamous proposal; and Matilda received her father's commands to be favourable to her generous suitor. I will not detail to you the persecutions which resulted from her firm refusal. The lover's father, irritated by her *obstinacy*, as he termed her *fortitude*, gave Sir Alexander to understand that he saw through the collusion, and that his daughter was taught her part by himself, in order to evade a connexion which his pride could not brook. Menaces followed; and he quitted the house, swearing that Sir Alexander should be roofless in a month. Intimidated by a threat which he well knew this man could effect, he became desperate in the means of avoiding it. The day of marriage was fixed, and Matilda was summoned from her prison chamber, to hear her fate from her father. She expostulated; he was deaf: she reminded him of his engagements with me; he sternly answered that she should not be a beggar; nor would he live to want bread; and bade her begone. 'Bless me before I go,' said she, meekly kneeling, 'send to me repose with a father's love.' The wretched parent, a stranger to the calmness of despair when at its climax, and viewing her tearless eye and collected features through the medium of his own wishes, raised her with transports of joy from her suppliant posture, and pouring out his fervent benedictions on her, he advised her to return to her apartment and compose her mind for the reception of her future husband and his father, who would, in the evening, convince her of the value they set on the alliance. She replied that she preferred a walk in the garden, and withdrew."—Sir Murdoch paused; he fixed his eyes on my face; they seemed covered with a dreadful film; he breathed short, and trembled as in an ague fit.—"For heaven's sake," exclaimed I, terrified, "let me give you something; you are ill."—He heard me not.—"Yes," said he, with a suppressed and tremulous voice, "she withdrew! and whither?—to the arms of mercy! Yes, she withdrew from opposition, from cruelty, to the bosom of her Redeemer! There was none to succour! none to help! When discovered, her vermilion cheek was pale! her eyes were closed! her beautiful tresses were mixed with the dank and filthy weeds of the stagnated pool! But her pure and unsullied soul had escaped pollution!"

"My dear Sir Murdoch," said I, "you distress me; for pity's sake, say no more. Let me call Lady Maclairn, indeed you grieve me, I cannot bear it." "Then how should I?" answered he; "yet I have survived her!"—He wiped away the tears which relieved him, and with more composure added, "be not alarmed, I am myself, and patient. My uncle," continued he, "lived only three weeks after this event. The destined bridegroom left the Highlands, and soon after died in his passage to the West Indies. His father was, I believe, consoled by adding Maclairn Castle and its impoverished demesnes to his possessions. I had, on quitting Scotland, taken with me as a domestic, my Matilda's foster brother. His sister, something older than himself, had been her favourite attendant; and the poor girl in the hour of this distress committed to Wallace the care of preparing me for this intelligence; advising him to chuse one of my friends for an office which she foresaw he would be unequal to. It appeared that the angel had preconcerted her design, before she attended her father's summons; she had affixed to my picture a scrap of paper, and placed them in Jenny's prayer book. This precious evidence of her love and truth was inclosed in Jenny's letter to her brother; and contained these words: 'I die, a Maclairn; and Maclairn's affianced, faithful Matilda.' The poor fellow, unable to stand the shock himself, rushed from the house with this fatal letter in his hand; and under such perturbation of mind that he had neither taken his hat, nor perceived that this slip of paper had escaped him. He sought my most intimate friend; and with agonies of grief implored his aid. In this interval of time, I, finding the summons of my bell unanswered, repaired to the room which Wallace occupied, and finding on his table the implements of writing, which I wanted, I sat down to write a card. Judging that he was not far remote, from seeing his hat; I moved it for my convenience. The note appeared! I will spare you, my child. Let it suffice, my friend and Wallace found me senseless. A raging fever succeeded. To this were opposed the cares of my friends, and a constitution never abused; but I was reduced to the state of an idiot; and as such, unconsciously embarked for England with my faithful Wallace, as unfit for the service, and from the hopes entertained of the change of climate and sea-air. He conducted me to his father's cottage; it was rich in nothing but fidelity and humanity; but in these, great Giver of all good! how liberal had been thy donation! Here the wretched Maclairn was received; and recovered his strength of body, and the faculty of knowing his misery. I sold my commission, paid my debts; and without a thought beyond my Matilda's grave, I laboured with my hosts for the bread we shared. Wallace, with patient love and unexampled attachment, had watched over my *despair*, my *feebleness*, my now *settled melancholy*. At length, he hazarded to speak of the recent rupture with our American colonies, and with a soldier's spirit he infused into my heart the wish of dying like one. I had still two or three hundred pounds left, and determined in my design, and apparently governed by his arguments to shake off the indolence which was destroying my life and my honour, I took the road he pointed out. On reaching London, Wallace soon established his claims to favour; and he embarked for America as serjeant with the first troops destined to subdue the malcontents of that country. My friends, advised me to wait for the result of their efforts in my favour, not thinking that I could with propriety serve in a subordinate rank to the one I had filled and quitted without disgrace. I consented; and took up my temporary residence in a lodging at Kensington-gravel-pits."

CHAPTER III

LETTER XXXV

"In this house I first met my Harriet. Her attractions were of a kind to engage my attention; for, like myself, she appeared to be the child of sorrow; and it was not difficult to discover that she was of a different order of beings from those who were with her. Her meek and pensive form, her tenderness to her infant, her courteous and unaffected manners when chance threw me in her way, soon produced their effects, and I insensibly forgot my usual train of thoughts in watching the hour for her appearing in our little garden with her nursling. She became interested for a man who, at this period, was again the prey of grief. I had intelligence of the death of my friend Wallace, who fell as honourably as he had lived. Her pity, her gentle soothings, drew from my overcharged bosom the whole tale of my woes. She wept, Miss Cowley; and told me that she also had known the pangs of *severed love* and *blasted hope*. Thus were our hearts cemented!

"For a time our union was opposed by her brother. I was poor; and in avowing my poverty Mr. Flamall perceived that I was proud. Miss Flint employed her influence in favour of Harriet's wishes; and on giving up my solicitations at the war office, our marriage took place without further opposition. My wife mentioned to me a promise she had made to Miss Flint, in consequence of her good offices with Mr. Flamall; and expatiating on her sister's, (as she styled her daughter in law,) fondness for her infant brother, she timidly proposed to me the plan of residing with Miss Flint at Tarefield Hall. I saw the mother in this arrangement; and I admitted the plea. Harriet was pleased, and Miss Flint was contented. On arriving here I found that every attention had been paid for securing my domestic comforts. Apartments were prepared for our exclusive use; and to do justice to Miss Flint, her conduct was at this period both discreet and generous. But my character was determined. I had found tranquillity: I had gained a heart on which to repose: my wife was my asylum from care; but I had no relish for joy: society was distasteful to me, and the common amusements of life were irksome and fatiguing. My Harriet, the kind and guardian angel that heaven had bestowed on me, convinced me that we were formed for each other. My tastes were hers, my comforts hers, and retirement was necessary to her happiness. I saw with contentment Miss Flint's increasing attachment to the little Philip: she was continually engaged in the nursery with him; and there appeared a perfectly good understanding established in our family. But this season of tranquillity was not permitted to be permanent. The birth of Malcolm, an event which had opened once more my mind to the sensations of joy, was marked for a source of petty discontents, and officious intrusions. Mr. Flamall's visits to the Hall became more frequent, and his stay longer. Lucretia, as my gentle Harriet told me with a languid smile, was jealous of the little stranger, and feared that she should love him. For a time this passed, but abstracted as I was in myself, and disposed as I had always been, to reserve with Mr. Flamall, I discovered that his presence was the signal for Harriet's depressed spirits and Miss Flint's peevishness. Struck from time to time by the insolent authority he held in the family, and the power he exercised over a woman impatient of the slightest contradiction from others, I was led to conclusions which could alone solve the difficulty; and I foresaw that the time was not remote when Miss Flint would have a tyrant legally authorized to be the despot at Tarefield. I mentioned my opinion to my wife; she acknowledged that she believed Lucretia loved her brother, but that she still loved her independence better; and the struggle, added she, has been for so long a time so equally maintained, that I think her temper and his own have gained nothing in the contest. He has, however, succeeded in gaining her confidence, by his zeal and knowledge in her business, and his partiality for her darling boy has confirmed in her a respect for his talents.

"Satisfied at length, that my temper would not conform to Mr. Flamall's growing influence, I determined on my measures of prudence; and mentioned to my wife my wish of residing in France, and particularly at Nismes, on account of the air, and from motives of economy. She cheerfully acceded to the proposal, and from that time became my pupil in the language of the country, rapidly recovering her school knowledge of it, and with improvement. But when my intention was declared to Miss Flint, my wife had to sustain a difficult part: prayers, reproaches, sullenness, and tears were employed to divert her from her compliance with my wishes and plan. She was firm, and steadily urged, that my health and spirits were objects which she could not, nor would not attempt to impede. Mr. Flamall was summoned from town, to assist in subduing Harriet's resolution. She referred him to me, and with all that poor and contemptible *cunning* which he calls *address*, he began his attack. He wondered what could have led me to the design of quitting a situation so convenient to my finances, and so congenial to my love of retirement. I answered with my usual reserve, that I had maturely deliberated on my plan, and should adhere to it. 'You have been *teased* into it,' answered he, 'by Harriet's silly complaints of the temper of Miss Flint. I think she has been wrong, for she has known her long enough not to mind the submissions she exacts from every one in her way.' 'Lady Maclairn has been hitherto silent with me on this point,' answered I; 'but I thank you for having given me an additional motive for leaving Tarefield. My wife shall not submit to the caprice or tyranny of any one whilst I can prevent her degradation.' He coloured. 'I perceive none in her conduct,' replied he, 'that is not enforced by her duty, as the mother of a child who has no father at hand to protect him. If she complies with the inequalities of this woman's temper, she will be well paid for her trouble; and I do not see how she can reconcile herself to her duty to her son Philip, by sacrificing his future expectations for an uncertain experiment. If she leave Philip with Miss Flint, her weak fondness will be his ruin; if she remove him, it is ten to one but that in a few months his place in her heart will be filled up by a new favourite; and she will hate him with the same fervour with which she at present conceives that his society is requisite to the preservation of her life.' 'He must take his chance, in this predicament,' replied I; 'and of two evils his mother will chuse the *least*. He will be rendered virtuous, I trust, by our cares, and he will escape the humiliating conditions annexed to dependence and expectations. I have no doubt of his mother's choice, nor will Miss Flint's fortune tempt her to leave her child to another's care.' He made no reply, and we parted. From this ineffectual trial of his eloquence, Mr. Flamall seemed convinced that I was not to be managed: he spoke no more on the subject. I had in the mean time, as I believed, silenced many of Miss Flint's fears. I had engaged to return in three years on a visit to Tarefield; and soothed her with the prospect of Philip's improvement, promising to be his tutor. She seemed to consider our departure as inevitable; and to experience the necessity of submitting with a good grace to a privation which she could not prevent. The first week in October was fixed for our leaving Tarefield; and September was given to our necessary preparations, and Lucretia's consolation."

Sir Murdoch paused for some moments: at length resuming his narrative, he said, "I am not quite certain, that what I have further to say is strictly conformable with my own notions of honour, or with that justice which is prescribed by our religion. My mind is prejudiced; my suspicions rest on conjectural ground; and you must listen to what follows with caution and candour. Believe, if it be possible, that my infirmity of mind has raised up the hideous spectre I am about to present to your eyes, and call it by any name but Flamall's" — He spoke with emotion, and wiped the faint dew from his forehead. "One evening in the early part of September," continued Sir Murdoch, "we were summoned from the avenue by the servant, who said that supper was served, and Mr. Flamall waiting for our return. I had, in conformity with Harriet's wishes, given more of my time than usual to Miss Flint, who had appeared sensible of my consideration. She pressed me to sup with her, and with good nature added, 'you will find your favourite ragout, which I ordered expressly for you.' I made no objections; and we entered the dining-room. Flamall was sitting at the spread table, reading a newspaper. 'I thought,' said he, throwing it aside, 'that I was doomed to sup solus; all has been waiting here these twenty minutes, and must now be cold.' 'Whose fault was that?' replied Miss Flint, taking her station. 'If you had not given *your orders*, the cook would have waited *for mine.*' 'I was half famished,' answered he, 'and a hungry man is not observant of ceremony.' During this observation he helped himself to the ragout of mushrooms, which stood at his hand, and with the eagerness of a keen appetite tasted them; when abruptly retiring to the side-board he regorged what he had taken, rinsed his mouth several times, and then swore, that one dish at least was hot enough for the devil himself. Knowing his aversion to spice, and particularly to Cayenne pepper, I was not disposed to condemn the cook, or to reject the mushrooms on his evidence; I therefore exchanged dishes with him, and helped myself to the reprobated mushrooms, and finding them seasoned to my palate, I ate some. He observed me, and remarked that he was astonished to see me relish so infernal a cookery. 'They are rather overdone,' said I, crossing my knife and fork, and asking for beer; 'but I have not yet done with them.' The awkwardness of the servant, or my haste, so managed the business, that the glass of beer fell, inundated my plate, and was shivered in a number of pieces among the mushrooms. Flamall cursed the servant; and my wife said she was glad of the disappointment I had received; for that she had been told, that in the great number of mushrooms apparently alike, there was only one sort wholesome. Order, however, was restored, and the spirit of contradiction gave place to more cheerful conversation.

"In the night I was suddenly seized with a violent pain and a severe nausea, which was somewhat relieved by warm water; languor and stupefaction succeeded to this effort of nature, and when the physician saw me, he pronounced my life doubtful, and called the malady a *putrid fever.* I was tempted to declare *my opinion of the disease* for I had heard *his*; but my wife was at my pillow. I soon became unconscious of my condition; *memory closed its records.*

"I will not attempt to describe to you, the sensations which assailed me, when I first recollected my wife. A sense of my own danger and of her protection were at once so blended that I could not for a moment support her absence. I was still persuaded that I had been poisoned; but my imagination had given a new form to Flamall. I thought it was a fiend invisible to all eyes but mine, and who watched to destroy my wife and child. His voice was for ever ringing in my ears—'They die if you discover me!' But let me quit a subject which unmans me, and afflicts you. Well might I have said, 'my kinsfolks have failed, and my familiar friends have forgotten me; they that dwell in mine house, and my maids, count me a stranger. I called my servant, and he gave me no answer.' One being only filled up this void, and that was *my Harriet*! Soothed by her gentleness, supported by her presence, my apartment was my world; and the horrors which had encompassed me gave place to passive quietness and transient pleasure, for my son Malcolm amused me. My recovery was slow and gradual; but in proportion as my reason gained strength, and my health was renewed, I experienced the painful sense of a mind conscious of its lost energies; and I considered myself as a subject for unfeeling curiosity, rather than for respect or usefulness. I shuddered with dread at the thoughts of being seen, and *for a time, no persuasion* could allure me into the garden. When, at length, I had in some degree recovered from this despondency, I listened with more docility to my wife's tender entreaties, and by degrees the garden became the boundary of my voluntary prison. Mr. Flamall's proposal of placing you here produced another change in my mind, for it roused in me a sense of injuries, and a resentment which bespoke a mind once more alive to its original character. I *will* leave England, said I to Malcolm, with an energy which astonished him. I will have no concerns with Mr. Flamall. His very name is abhorrent to my ears. *He is a villain!* I checked myself; and Malcolm, to my surprise, said with calmness, 'I have long known him as one. But if *Maclairn* can prevent the mischief he is now meditating, will he not exert his prerogative? My father is made for the agent of Providence in the cause of the oppressed.' He proceeded to inform me of the circumstances relative to you, which had reached him by means of a young friend. The result of this conversation you know. I was resolved to receive you, to guard you from a less eligible situation, and in a word to shelter innocence, as securely as I could, from the machinations of a man, who I have reason to believe to be as cruel as he is artful and designing. Deprived as you are, my dear young lady," continued the worthy creature, "of those pleasures which youth demands, and of the society of your early friends, yet, believe me, you are not without a guardian here: my arm, were it necessary, should protect you; and in a just cause, it would yet be found a *Maclairn's*." His dark blue eyes were again fixed on my face, but with what expression!—"Not even my Harriet's claims," added he, "would restrain my vengeance, were my Matilda's image insulted."

"I neither fear Mr. Flamall's power, nor have I submitted to his authority," replied I, "in choosing to withdraw from my friend Mr. Hardcastle's house." My heart was on my lips, Lucy, and I briefly related to him my motives. "But," continued I, "little did I expect to find a parent in any abode appointed by such a miscreant as Flamall. I joyfully accept of the endearing title you offer: call me your child, your daughter: your affection shall be returned in acts of duty and reverence." "And when you forsake us," said he, relapsing into pensiveness, "what are we to do?" "To rejoice in my happiness," answered I, "to solace your declining years with your Malcolm's children and mine; to live an evidence of that truth which promises peace to the virtuous man, both *here* and *hereafter*." — "It is her blessed spirit which speaks," said he. — "I will not permit you, my dear father," answered I, "to indulge in this enthusiasm; let us call a new subject." "I will obey you," replied he, "after one question. Tell me, has it not been a matter of surprise to you, as well as of curiosity, to see my wife so much influenced and attached to Miss Flint?" "Yes," replied I with firmness; "but your story has solved the enigma; Lady Maclairn knows that her brother has been, and may be still dear to this woman, and the sister's humanity wishes to repair the mischief which the brother's infidelity has made." He looked pleased. "It may be so," observed he, "for I know her principles." His wife at this instant entered, and with assumed gaiety I told her, that I had been making my confession to Sir Murdoch, in return for his adopting me as a daughter. She smiled, and answered that she hoped I was also disposed to receive her as a mother. I gave her my hand, but added, "Will you be indulgent? Will you, like my father, permit me to love the man whom my heart and my understanding have prefered? On no other condition will I promise to be your *dutiful daughter*." "Receive the blessing on any terms, my dear Harriet," said the baronet, pressing our hands in his; "she has already shed peace into my bosom, and hope and comfort into yours." Lady Maclairn made no other reply, than that of hiding her face in my bosom, and weeping.

Again, Lucy, do I repeat for the thousandth time, that *all is not genuine in this woman's conduct*. There is a *something* which pervades and obstructs the display of those feelings which nature has bestowed on her, as intended blessings to herself and others, and with which she appears perpetually to struggle. At one moment her heart seems to be on her very lips with me; at another, she is silent, and as though intimidated by my presence. Sometimes I fancy my frankness is obtrusive, and my manners too unceremonious. I become more attentive, and she appears serious and more pensive, and anxiously inquires whether I am displeased with her. My answer dissipates the apprehension; cheerfulness returns, till some unguarded expression, some casual incident, again impedes my access to her heart. I think, Lucy, that she would not be a sufferer were she to trust me: I am certain that my compassion is now the most active of my feelings. She imagines, perhaps, that I think her a sharer in her brother's plots and contrivances; but she is mistaken, for I know that she has detested him from the hour he proposed sending her husband to a mad-house; and I am assured, that she has not the most remote suspicion of his having in any way been accessary to Sir Murdoch's illness; for she has more than once told me, that his complaint came on as gradually as it has disappeared, and originated in the catastrophe of his cousin's death. I must finish this subject. Mrs. Allen assures you that Miss Cowley is well, and that her nightly dreams are not disturbed by *scarlet fevers*.

Heaven bless you, and all I love at Heathcot!

Rachel Cowley.

LETTER XXXVI

From the same to the same.

As you are become reasonable, Lucy, I will tell you that Doctor Douglas is still of opinion, that I am better in the house than I should be by another buffeting from the north wind, to which he principally ascribes my late indisposition. My saline draughts, however, have now given place to orange jelly, which, as it pleases the *pet*, Mrs. Allen makes according to her recipe. She left me this morning to replenish her store, and Mrs. Warner's little parlour being convenient for the purpose, the cookery was done there; the kind hearted Mrs. Warner aiding and assisting. "I wish," said she, "I could persuade my lady to exchange her taste for rum and water, for this pleasant and refreshing jelly; I am sure it would be better for her: she is in a constant fever; and what with her poor leg, and her fretting, she is hourly sinking." Mrs. Allen expressed her concern. "You would indeed pity her," replied Warner, "if you knew all: she is, at times, the most miserable creature in the world; and between ourselves, I think she is losing her senses. That was *a warning voice*, Mrs. Allen, that reached her from the poor captain, the last time he was in this house, or I am much mistaken. I have heard that Miss Flint was very unkind to her sister, Mrs. Howard, and the captain roused her *sleeping conscience*. I have lived with her nine years, and I can safely say that she is a changed woman in less than nine weeks. She has of late taken it into her head to send me to bed before her, and I hear her for hours after walking about her room. Within the last fortnight she has been writing all day, and rummaging in her cabinet for letters, which she burns by dozens: then again, her temper madam, is now quite altered; for I do assure you she is as patient as a lamb! and if you could but see her knee, you would never forget it. I am sure it makes me tremble to see how she suffers." "Why do you not persuade her to have more able advice than her apothecary's?" observed Mrs. Allen. "Bless you, my dear madam!" replied she, "Lady Maclairn has almost on her bended knees begged her to consult Doctor Douglas, with whom she is so pleased; but she will not consent. She says, 'Do not urge me; *you know, Harriet, that no doctor can cure me.* I must bear with patience this visitation of the Almighty,' and then she weeps for hours."

You know Mrs Allen, and you will not be surprised to hear that she has seen the miserable invalid this morning; whom she found much more changed than even Warner's report had led her to expect. To-morrow I am to dine with the Heartleys: my doctor is the promoter of this enlargement, and will be here to see me properly equipped for the coach. I mean to be docile, for I expected this morning that Mrs. Patty, our maid, would have laid violent hands on me, for daring to cross the hall without clogs and my shawl. Be cheerful, my Lucy. I have to write to our Horace: and remember when you write from Heathcot, the words of the poet: "Where ignorance is bliss 'tis folly to be wise." Not a word of my *dreadful scarlet fever*, He might fancy fiction were truth, and that your Rachel Cowley had really been in danger of death, and of thus cheating him *of a wife to rule.*

Your's, as truly as *his,*

R. Cowley.

P. S. The unavoidable delay of my friend's dispatches permits me to add to the bulk of my letter. Leaving to the lovers of the pathetic and sublime at the abbey to describe my "secret interesting languor," and "fascinating" pale face, I shall simply tell you, that what with a hearty dinner on Mrs. Wilson's boiled fowls, and as hearty a welcome, they sent me home with a different complexion, and as blythe as a bird.

On entering the parlour, we found Lady Maclairn alone; and for once counterfeiting failed, for her eyes were swoln with weeping. Sir Murdoch with tender alarm asked, "What had happened to distress her." "Wherefore do you ask that question, sir?" demanded Malcolm, with emotion. "Is it not always from one and the same cause that my mother stands indebted for her trials of patience?" "If you mean poor Lucretia," answered she with mildness, "you wrong her, at least on this occasion, for I have scarcely seen her to-day: she was engaged in writing. But what will you say, when I tell you that I have to thank *Miss Cowley* for my red eyes?" She smiled affectionately on me, and added that I had left the new play of the *Stranger* in her way, "and if such be Kotsebue's influence on the passions," observed she, "in a foreign garb, what must be the effect he produces in his own language! I have been deeply interested in the piece." "I lose my patience continually," replied I, "when I think of the hours of comfort and amusement you give up to the silly resentment of an unreasonable woman. Why do you not cease being a *stranger* to your neighbours? Mrs. Heartley is formed for your friend." "I am never so happy, as *at home*," replied she, interrupting me. "I have my blessings under this roof, habit has endeared it to me; and at present, Heaven be praised! it is my own fault if I be not happy." She fondly leaned on her husband's shoulder as she said this. Malcolm placing himself in the vacant space on the other side on the sofa, observed, with seriousness, that contentment, at least, was in her reach; for that Mr. Wilson had secured the refusal of the *Wereland Farm;* and could either purchase the estate, or have it on a long lease. "I am rejoiced to hear you are likely to succeed," replied she, "for from your description of its beauties it must be an enviable spot." "To me it would be a *paradise* under any description," replied the son, "could I promise myself to see you and my father inmates with me there. A cottage with mud walls and independence is all I wish." "You are right, my dear Malcolm," answered she, with dignity. "But do not imagine your mother is a slave beneath this roof. You give to the little vexations of my life, much more importance than I do. Poor Lucretia may, it is true, sometimes appear to you capricious and imposing, and thus disturb the serenity you wish me; but I am weak whenever this happens, for I know she loves me; and whilst she lives I shall never have a wish to quit Tarefield." "Would to God, then, she were dead!" said Malcolm. "You would be more charitable," answered she, mildly, "did you better understand her present condition." "Perhaps I might," replied he, "and wish her reformation, could I believe the Ethiopian could change his skin." "There needs no miracle to effect a reformation of our tempers, Malcolm," said she gravely; "the attempt is arduous, the path is difficult which leads to repentance; but it is not inaccessible; and if you knew the present difficulties of this poor woman, labouring under sickness and dejection of mind, you would not wish that the only friend she has *on earth* should quit her." Malcolm was silenced; and if such be the motives of Lady Maclairn's conduct *I* ought to be silenced.

At supper Mrs. Allen joined us; she had prevailed on the invalid to call in Doctor Douglass, who to-morrow is to meet her former physician, *a Doctor Tufton*. Her account of Miss Flint softened the good Baronet; but I perceived that Malcolm's prejudices were unconquered. Mrs. Allen tells me this woman is dreadfully ill; and suffers excruciating pain from the tumour on her knee. Like Malcolm my hour of conversion is not yet arrived; and if pain and sickness are necessary to her salvation, why should I grieve? Yet one does not like to hear of remedies that are worse than horse-whipping. Good night, my dear girl! Allen is weary, and I am on my good behaviour still; for Douglass is offended by my late hours; and swears he will write to Mr. Hardcastle and prevent your letters, "tempting me to evil." Tell Mary every one here loves her, and that her sister boasts of her. You will add whatever will content you to the name of

Rachel Cowley.

The reader is now to be informed that Miss Cowley's pen was for more than a month suspended by a visit which Miss Hardcastle and Miss Howard made at the Abbey. The termination of Miss Cowley's minority, as settled by law, put her into possession of her grandmother's fortune; and counsellor Steadman was induced, partly with a view to that business, and partly to consult his fair client in respect to a letter written by Mr. Flamall on the subject of his nephew's secret marriage, to pay her a short visit. The young ladies were therefore conducted by him to Mr. Wilson's; and their escort home was the counsellor's friend, whose house at Bishop's Auckland was his abode during his stay.

It appears that Mr. Flamall acknowledged that the restrictive clauses in Mr. Cowley's will relative to his daughter's marrying M. Philip Flint were rendered null and void by the impossibility of her acceding to the conditions; but he insisted on his right to the exercise of his office not only as this related to the management of her property, but also to her choice of a husband. With many law arguments he proved that Miss Cowley could not marry without his consent till she had attained her twenty-fifth year, without incurring the disability declared in her father's will for her unconditional possession of his property. "You, Sir," continues he, "will, as a professional man, see, that, were I more disposed than I am to forego a trust committed to me by a friend whom I still revere, the law would oblige me to do my duty. Were it not so, believe me I would cheerfully relinquish an office which neither suits my health nor gratifies my feelings. I am not ignorant of Miss Cowley's unjust suspicions of my *honour*, nor of the prejudicies she has infused into the minds of her friends. My conduct shall be a full refutation of the charges she has brought against me; charges which originated from the disappointment of her romantic views; and from too implicit a confidence in those to whose care she had been incautiously trusted." He next entered into the detail of his nephew's ingratitude, &c. but as the reader is prepared for this subject and, it may be, disposed in favour of youthful indiscretion, rather than to sympathise in Mr. Flamal's mortifications, I shall pass over this part of the letter, which concludes with mentioning his intention of conducting the two young Cowleys to England in the following spring, in order to place them in a more suitable situation, than with their mother, at Mr. Dalrymple's.

Miss Cowley's friends still adhered to their first opinion, and Mr. Flamall was suffered to remain in his post without other marks of distrust than such as the counsellor's vigilance and the attention of Miss Cowley's friend, Mr. Oliver Flint, gave to his mode of conduct. But Mr. Flamall wanted not for acuteness; and, foiled in his ambition, he thought it prudent to secure a safe retreat. Fortunately for himself, as well as for Miss Cowley's interest, he found for once, that "honesty was the best policy:" that by employing his talents and his diligence for the benefit of the estates he might succeed in gaining a good report, and the continuance of an employment which was advantageous and respectable.

Sir Murdoch during this term of jubilee, as it might be called at Tarefield, found other faces to admire as well as Miss Cowley's. His contentment rose to cheerfulness, and in the enjoyment of a society whose attention and solicitude were given to please and amuse him, he so entirely gained the advantage over his habits of retirement and his dejection of mind, that in Miss Cowley's words, "she had ceased to love him, for he had the nerves and activity of a fox-hunter." Miss Flint's declining health and spirits were the two ostensible apologies for Lady Maclairn's taking no part in these hours of cheerfulness and social ease. She succeeded in her request that Miss Hardcastle would divide her time between the Abbey and the Hall; and Lucy, with a candour and gentleness so peculiarly her own, was not only charmed with her, but with unceasing labour endeavoured to remove from her friend the prejudices she entertained to her disadvantage. Mrs. Allen, ever on the side of charity, took up Miss Hardcastle's arguments; and Miss Cowley, with her natural frankness, acknowledged that her being Mr. Flamall's sister might have biassed her judgment. Some steps were taken to produce a reconciliation between the captain and Miss Flint: these were made without his knowledge, for Miss Flint refused to see her niece; and Lady Maclairn judged it improper to urge her request; as it appeared the subject distressed her, and increased her melancholy.

The departure of the young ladies in the beginning of June, again leaves me to my allotted task; and my readers to the gratification of their curiosity.

LETTER XXXVII

From Miss Cowley to Miss Hardcastle.

Be comforted, my dear girl. We are trying at the Abbey to forget you, and to be contented with *every-day* blessings. Mr. Hardcastle and Mr. Sedley are now enjoying their holidays. And I hope that Mary's April face is exchanged for one which their kind greetings will render cheerful. As you may both of you have some compunction hanging about you, for having disturbed the tranquillity of Tarefield, I will inform you, that fortune, liking Sir Murdoch's holiday face better than that of *Malvolio*, which, in the days of my folly, I wickedly gave him, has by one of those freaks so common in her administration, produced a letter, which has dissipated the gloom your absence caused, and he has been laughing with me at the contents. Here followeth a copy for your edification.

LETTER XXXVIII

To Lady Maclairn, from Mrs. Serge.

Putney, June the 9th.

"My dear cousin."

This letter will surprise you I dare say; and, it may be, puzzle you, unless you remember your giddy Lydia Hatchway; but old love with me is not forgot, though so many years have passed since we last met. However, I doubt not but as Mrs. Serge, you will still acknowledge your former friend; and trusting to this hope, I sat down to inform you of my intentions to renew the hintercourse so long interrupted by various hevents. The bad state of health of my eldest girl have, for a long time, been a great affliction to Mr. Serge as well as myself. We have tried Bath, and consulted several doctors without gaining any advantage. We are now advised by a very clever young man, whom my Jerry meets frequently at his horacle's, a Counsellor Steadman's, to trust to her youth and change of air; and it is determined that this summer shall be given to journeying. Thank God, my Jerry is a hindependent man, having given up business, with a very *heasy* fortune, so we have no cares about *hexpences*; but we have been for a time quite undetermined in regard to the road we should take. I was for the *tower* of Norfolk; but I have been out-voted. My daughter Nora, who has just left her school in —— square, talkes much of the beauties of *Vales*, and have bought a set of prints to shew us; but I am not willing to leave England, and with a sick person it vould be very improper to go to a place vhere the people do not understand English; so Vales is out of the question. But Nora talks much, at present, of some lakes in your part of the world, which it seems, are *wisited* by every person of taste; and although I never heard of them before, I am much inclined to indulge her with a sight of them, as I can, at the same time, gratify my wish of seeing your ladyship. My husband highly approve of this plan; but fear that you will not relish so many *hintruders,* even for a night or two; but I tell him I am certain you will welcome us as *hold* friends if you can make it convenient to lodge us. We shall travell slow, on account of Caroline and our horses; and rest with you a day or two. You may expect to see us, bag and baggage, about the end of this month; but I shall hope to hear from you before we finally determine on our journey, and in case our wisit suit you, will give you notice of our happroach before you see us. With compliments to Sir Murdoch and Mr. Maclairn,

I remain
Your affectionate cousin and friend,

Lydia Serge.

P.S. We shall bring a maid with us. Counsellor Steadman assure my Jerry that you will not find it difficult to provide for our horses. We shall have six with us, besides the servants', that run *hout*: my husband is only afraid, that you will think we are taking a freedom that may give not only trouble but offence; but I laugh at his scruples; for you well know, I expect no ceremony, nor practice none with those I love.

  I have really, my dear Lucy, exerted my utmost skill, in copying Mrs. Serge's epistle *verbatim*; but I was never more convinced of the truth contained in the wise man's observation, "Train up a child in the way he should go," says the son of Sirach, "and when he is old he will not depart from it." My fingers and talents have been so long cramped by my first spelling book, that I much doubt whether I have done justice to Mrs. Serge's orthography; but when she arrives I will study her vocabulary, in order to prove to Mary that she has still to learn a language which she may need without losing sight of British land. With streaming eyes, for laughter has its tears, I *"himplored"* Lady Maclairn to *"hadmit"* these guests. She did more than smile; for laughing in her turn, she asked Sir Murdoch whether he was disposed to indulge his daughter with the opportunity of acquiring a language, which, with my gaiety, and its novelty, would render me irresistible. He answered cheerfully that he had only one fear; and that was, lest such an addition to her cares should be fatiguing to herself, and, it might be, unpleasant to Miss Flint. "I have no apprehensions," replied she mildly: "as to Lucretia's consent," her features reassuming their usual pensiveness, and that suspicion succeeding, which it has been yours and Mrs. Allen's labour to convince me proceeds from timidity and delicate nerves; "I have no doubts of my sister Lucretia's perfect acquiescence," added she; "and I confess it would gratify me to acquit myself of a part of that debt of gratitude which I owe to this lady's aunt, who by her attentions and tender care of me, probably, saved my life: her father and mother also were extremely kind to me when I was with them, and, as was supposed, far gone in a decline." "Then lose no time, my Harriet," answered the baronet, "in acquainting her, that we shall receive them as friends; and that we will do all we can do for the accommodation of *friends*." She looked pleased, but hesitated. "I have yet one point to settle before I determine," observed she. "Mr. Serge is a plain honest man; but he is little acquainted with the usages of the world. His wife, I presume, has not gained much improvement of mind since I knew her: although in a prosperous situation of fortune, we may, I think, conclude that her society has not been select. You will find these people quite remote from yourself; they will be troublesome to you, and if my cousin Lydia likes Tarefield, she may delay her visit to the lakes rather longer than you will relish: I am certain they will not amuse you." Sir Murdoch eagerly set aside this objection. All is now *en train* for Mrs. Serge's reception; for Lady Maclairn has sent off her answer, and cordial acceptance of the visit; and preparations are now making for their arrival.

In continuation.—For once, at least, in my life I will do justice to Lady Maclairn's address. She has been to consult me on the means her fertile genius has adopted to *trick* Sir Murdoch into another apartment. Our plot has succeeded, and we are now busy in making such arrangements for him, as will, it is hoped, soon reconcile him to the loss of his detestable grated windows, and which will tend to obliterate from his mind the saddening ideas associated with his prison. This apartment is now to be destined to the strangers' use, and they will have but one staircase to explore to their several rooms. I have also been prepared to form my estimate of the pleasure I may expect from our visitors. She spoke of Mrs. Serge's parents. Captain Hatchway was the master of a ship, and his family resided at Y—m—th. His sister, Mrs. Priscilla Hatchway, had been the early friend of Lady Maclairn's mother, and was her first cousin. "I have not seen Mrs. Serge, for many years," added her ladyship. "She was then a thoughtless, giddy girl, but perfectly innocent and good natured. When she lost her good father, I have reason to believe she had little whereon to depend for her future maintenance: her mother had no talents for economy, and her daughter's union with Mr. Serge was a circumstance of great utility to her, as well as of security to her lively and pretty daughter. Mr. Serge was rich when he married, and since that time has been very fortunate, by an accession of wealth which he little expected. He is a worthy honest man; and as she says, a *hexcellent* husband, though more than twenty years her senior; but you may imagine that neither his education nor his pursuits in life can have any similarity with Sir Mordoch's. He has been 'Mr. Serge the rich taylor' till within these three or four years, when I heard that he had dropped this designation, for 'Mr. Serge the *contractor;*' now, it appears, he is 'Mr. Serge the *gentleman;*' and it is only to be feared, that his lady will find more difficulty in sustaining this part, than any which she has hitherto performed. She will have gained little, if the simplicity of her character has been infringed by her commerce with fashion and luxury; for her spirits, when I knew her, were extremely volatile." I was left: the workmen summoning her ladyship, who is at present very busy in Sir Murdoch's deserted prison. New hangings, new windows, &c. are to change its aspect. Sir Murdoch, either discomfited by seeing the alterations which have taken place in his fortress, or vexed that his wife has converted her dressing-room to his convenience, has been with me in his turn; and with some signs of spleen, he observed, that Harriet would have matters settled in her own way; for she never regarded what was due to herself. "I could have done very well without my apartment for a week," added he, "and without dispossessing her of a room she likes; and I suppose these good people will not stay longer than a few days; for I think they will soon be tired of us." "I hope not," answered I, "for I expect much amusement from them." "A few hours will lessen your enjoyment," replied he gravely, "of any amusement which makes no appeal to your taste and understanding: you will not find in novelty an equivalent for ignorance and vulgarity. As for the husband of our cousin, I am prepared to find in him one of those characters which more peculiarly disgust me; for unless he has more modesty and common sense than the generality of that class of men who are elevated by wealth to stations which neither their birth nor attainments in knowledge can make easy to them, he will soon weary me. I understand he has already dropped the *taylor* for the *contractor*; and, without doubt, fancies himself qualified to rank with any of his superiors." I saw that the blood royal of Malcolm King of Scotland, or at least of the Highlanders, was not exhausted by flowing through the veins of Sir Murdoch and his progenitors for so many centuries. It mounted to his face; and I should have smiled saucily, had I not recollected the pure reservoir it filled in the baronet's bosom. I can pardon this childish vanity, Lucy, when I see it qualified by an honest pride; and if by a consciousness of the eminence of our ancestors, in the annals of time, which blazon forth their glory and virtue, we be emulated to follow in the same track, it is well. But in Sir Murdoch I regard with lenity even a little pride of heart for the *shadow* of greatness; any thing which gives to him *self-consequence,* and *self-confidence* is useful to him, as tending to repress the painful recollection of those hours, when by his malady, he was levelled lower than the dust; and under which the boasted prerogatives of man, and all the adventitious circumstances of his place in this world, are sunk in darkness! A little vanity will not hurt my patient; and it is the pleasure of my life here, to see that I can make him laugh at my follies, and forget his own infirmities. Farewell!

Yours, faithfully,

Rachel Cowley.

P. S. The Heartleys, with their beaux left us yesterday. Poor Malcolm wishes the Serges had taken the unknown route to "Vales." "But man is born to trouble." He could not leave his father to the burden of Mr. Serge. Heaven preserve you! We are well; and the domestic arrangements necessary for our expected visitors have been useful to Lady Maclairn—*She thinks less.*

LETTER XXXIX

From Miss Cowley to Miss Hardcastle.

July the 1st.

"To journalise, to send the whole and full length pictures of the Serges," such are my Lucy's commands. "To be faithful in detailing the conversation of Mrs. Serge," *Voilà* Mary, who adds, that "a new language is so delightful when from her dear Miss Cowley's mouth or pen!" Next comes Mr. Hardcastle: your father, Lucy, can bribe, can cajole. True to his sex, he still knows the direct road to a woman's heart. But it may be that you, who are on some points an obstinate unbeliever, may demand *proofs* of his *savoir faire* with your simple-hearted Rachel. I will transcribe his little and *well-sealed* note for your conviction. "My dear *child*, I send you a model, by which you are in future to make up your letters for Heathcot. The gentleman, who brought me the dispatches from Lisbon which I now forward to you, has filled my heart with joy and hope. *Your brother Horace* was the subject of his conversation for an hour; and we must love him, my child, for he is beloved wherever he is known. When my kind visitor quitted me, I proceeded to examine the parcel he had left; which, from its rotundity, I judged to be a Portugal onion. It remains for you to investigate the truth of my supposition; for on examination, I found only the first *"peeling"* was destined for *Heathcot*. You will therefore be graciously disposed to indemnify us for the unequal partition of Horace's gift; and send us the *shreds, trimmings,* and even the *pack-thread* which you will glean from the respectable society of Mr. Serge's family. I love my girl in her sportive humour; and never think of her without losing a portion of my own!"

With my heart on my lips, and the Portugal onion in my bosom, can you blame me if I should transgress your law of charity, Lucy? I will be as good as I can; but thus tempted to folly, if I sin thank my betrayer, and do not chide me.

Yesterday we were all prepared for our guests' appearance at the dining hour. I kept my station at the dressing-room window, being too happy to be good company below stairs. Suppose you place yourselves by my side. But no: that idea would have spoiled me for an observer of all beyond the walls of the room whereas I was on the *alert*. First then, drew up a handsome plain coach, with nothing beyond Mr. Serge's modest cypher on its highly finished pannels: it was drawn by four beautiful bright bay horses, driven by two postillions in plain dark green livery jackets. This equipage was followed by an elegant and low phaeton; the horses making the set, as I presume, being exactly like the others. Two out-riders, well mounted, completed the cavalcade. So much for the *Taylor*'s first approach, which wanted only glare and ostentation to rival a *Nabob*'s. Mr. Serge slowly and cautiously alighted, "round as the shield of my fathers." (Sir Murdoch sees not my profanation of Ossian's sublimity). He was soberly dressed in a complete suit of dark brown broad-cloth, a *wig*—(you know my veneration for wigs,) which, had it been properly distributed, would have supplied crops for a regiment of spruce journeymen, and brainless coxcombs. A large silk handkerchief tied loosely round his neck; plain and homely features, with a healthy cheek and treble chin. In defiance of all given rules, Mr. Serge's leg and foot are admirably neat and well formed; and though neither decorated with silk stockings nor fashionable buckles, more than rivals *Mr. Snughead*'s.

His greetings with the baronet were unconstrained and hasty; for he instantly advanced to the phaeton, in which rode the poor Caroline the picture of youth subdued by sickness; and nearly exhausted by fatigue and weak spirits. She called upon me for compassion, and I forgot your orders, whilst contemplating her languid countenance. The father, unmindful of all but her, was preparing to assist her, when Malcolm saying something to her, took her in his arms and carried her into the drawing-room, Mr. Serge following him. Next appeared Mrs. Serge in a light green habit; her fair and round face heightened to the milk-maid's hue by the closeness of the carriage: a profusion of ringlets, well filled with brown powder, but which had maliciously quitted the station assigned it, and then lodged on all the *prominent* parts of Mrs. Serge's person, leaving the golden locks deprived of their glossy brightness, though not their colour: an embroidered waistcoat, lappelled, and more open at the bosom than even fashion of late has sanctioned: this deficiency was supplied by lace and cambrick; gold earrings and necklace, a riding hat and feathers; and in a hand, garnished with rings, and as white as snow, she carried a parasol. Her voice loud; her utterance flippant, and her salutation familiar and loquacious. Next, lightly sprang from the carriage the beautiful Leonora, the youngest daughter, her dark brown locks hanging in disorder over the face of a wood nymph; large and intelligent dark eyes, and a cheek vying in colour with the autumnal peach: the lightness of a sylph and the grace of fashionable ease. The loud laugh which reached me from Mrs. Serge did not prevent me seeing *Miss Lydia* emerge from her concealment. She very deliberately gave to Sir Murdoch a little black terrier to hold, and with a piece of cake in her hand, as deliberately secured her footing on terra-firma; but she was slip-shod, and caution was necessary. In size she comes very near to her mother, and she would be as pretty, were she not too pale. The golden locks are with Miss Lydia softened down to flaxen-coloured, which, with very light blue eyes, give an expression of heaviness to her countenance, perfectly conformable to her fat, and square person. Next and last came a smart abigail, and Miss Lydia hastily seizing her arm, followed the steps of Sir Murdoch and the ladies into the house.

I remained in my apartment, till summoned by Malcolm to his mother. I learned, that Miss Serge had nearly fainted before she reached the drawing-room, that she had retired to her own room, but was recovered. My introduction to the strangers followed, and I took my seat. The dustiness of the roads, and apologies for Mrs. Serge's being in such a "pickle," succeeded to the compliments of my entrance; "but as *Villet* was busy about Caroline, she was compelled to *haccept* of her ladyship's *hindulgence*, and remain as she was: but I think, child," added she, turning to Miss Nora, "you might make yourself a little more tidy; I dare say Miss Cowley would lend you *a comb*." My offers of service were prevented by the young lady's saying pertly, that she trusted also to Lady Maclairn's good-nature for an excuse, not knowing the secret of being *tiddy*, without an entire change of dress. The broad stare at me from time to time, the weary, careless attention to what was addressed to herself, at once spoke the *girl of fashion*. I took out my netting box, and the young lady, after curiously examining some books on a side table, withdrew into the bow window and read. Do you wish me to speak as loud and fast as Mrs. Serge? recollect that I have her dialect to acquire, and that I have not a speaking trumpet at command, but I will do my best. To the detail of her daughter's long illness, who had taken all "*mander* of shings," and tried a *hocean* of physic, succeeded "*hold*" stories of her father and mother, in which her filial tenderness unaffectedly appeared, and to which Lady Maclairn gave a lively interest by adding her testimony to their worth. "My dear mother had an excellent constitution, and the best spirits in the world," observed Mrs. Serge: "even *ater* she was a *vidow*, she could tire out two or three partners in a night's dancing; but, dear soul! she trusted too much to her strength, and refusing to change her clothes after being wet to the skin in a *water frolic*, she never held up her head." Tears fell copiously from Mrs. Serge's eyes in this part of the conversation, but in a few minutes the cloud gave place to a hearty laugh, on recollecting Mr. Flamall's cheating her with a painted "vindow at the castle at *Vindsor*, so *naturally done* that no soul alive would have taken it for a painted *vone*." Questions and wonderments succeeded, that so handsome a man had not made his *fortin* by marrying; she was sure it had been his own fault. Lady Maclairn soon changed this topic by asking her how she liked Bath. "Why on the whole *wery vell*," replied she, "but it is not to be compared with *Lunnun*: the rooms are certainly *wery* grand, but it is *halways* the same thing. I like to see a play, or Sadler's Wells much better; and as for the Criscent, and the Circus, in some *vinds*, you would think yourself in Y——th Downs in a *northheaster*; but one see *swarms* of fine folks come from the hupper part of the town, to bask in the sun on the South Parade, where we had our lodgings." Willing to hear the sound of the beauty's voice, and as willing to spare the further distension of her rosebud mouth, I asked her whether the season for Bath had been full. "Much as usual," replied she; "there were many people of rank and fashion, but we had few opportunities of meeting with them. Good society depends on a proper introduction." She threw on her mother a glance, which I could not misunderstand. "As for *hintroduction*, Nora," observed the good Mrs. Serge, "I found that *wery* heasy; you have only to shew your purse, and you may have a card party when you please. I could have been acquainted with several ladies of quality, if I would have played the new fashioned way at loo, but," continued she, addressing herself to Lady Maclairn, "I was soon sick of *pam* when he was in *good company*, as they call themselves. I was not cunning enough for your Lady Gudgeons; nor you, child, for her saucy daughters." Miss Nora had not time to reply to her share of the last observation. The mother continued—"Who do you think I saw at Bath, finer than our princesses? But you will never guess! Don't you remember the pretty little girl who used to sing to you at my aunt Prissy's? I mean the Knacker's daughter. She is now the wife of a very rich man, and is quite the fashion. I took an opportunity of reminding her of old friends and former times; she drew up, forsooth! and *wery* coldly observed that I had a *wery* good memory! She had been so long in the world, that she had forgotten me, till I announced my name. I detest pride, my lady, so I was resolved to be even with her. 'Dear me!' said I, 'I wonder how people can forget early friends. I have often thought of you and the scrape you got into, by breaking three or four "quarrels" in Mrs. Doughty's parlour window. My dear mother often used to laugh at the fright you were in, when she pacified the old lady, by paying the damage you had done, and saving you from being put in the cellar.' She looked," added the speaker, laughing heartily, "as though she would have preferred Mrs. Doughty's cellar to my conversation. But I have no notion of a little prosperity turning one's head, 'tis a poor return to make for God's goodness."

Miss Nora, during this discourse, had relapsed into silence, and was endeavouring to find amusement by poring over some music books she had taken up. "You play, no doubt," observed I; "and I have a harp, and a good piano-forte in my apartment." She smiled bewitchingly. "A *little* on both these instruments," answered she, "but I am out of practice, for I am no Orpheus, and cannot give to stocks and stones the power of feeling the charms of music." A summons to the dining-room prevented my reply. We there found the gentlemen and Miss Lydia, who, "*malgré elle*," soon completed the family party. "How is Miss Serge?" asked Lady Maclairn, in a tone of tenderness so peculiarly her endowment; "I hope she has slept, otherwise I should not be able to pardon myself for not being with her." "Poor thing!" replied the father, "she was better with me, for she is so flurried, and so fearful of being troublesome here, that it has made her very poorly indeed." "We will soon make her well, my good sir," replied the baronet, "if she has no malady more serious than this: my Harriet will soon convince her that she is at home." "Thank ye, Sir Murdoch," answered the agitated father. "I have no doubts on the subject, and I told my dear girl I was sure you were not of the number of those who think a sick guest a burden. God forbid it should be so! for such must needs have hard hearts! But Willet tells us," continued he, addressing his daughter Lydia, "that your sister was frightened, and disturbed last night: why did you not call me up? You know it is what I desire you to do always, when she does not settle." "Lord, papa!" replied Miss Lydia, "it was nothing but a drunken man in the next chamber who was *obstroperous*. I told her twenty times that our door was bolted. He might have *fit* with the other *feller* till sunrise, they would not have kept me from sleeping if Caroline had been quiet." "Mr. Serge has fully accounted for your sister's indisposition to-day," observed Lady Maclairn mildly; "you have good health, my dear young lady, and do not know how soon the weak are fluttered; but a night of undisturbed repose will remedy, I trust, this little alarm." Poor Lydia blushed, but did not answer. "I expect to establish my credit as a Lady Bountiful, before you leave me," continued Lady Maclairn, with assumed cheerfulness, turning to Mrs. Serge; "I have not forgotten your aunt Priscilla's recipes, which saved me from a decline, nor the kindness with which she administered them: it would be to me a blessing to imitate her in her tender cares." Mr. Serge crossed his knife and fork, and fixed his tearful eyes on Lady Maclairn's face, whilst his lady cordially thanked her, and added, "But you must try also to persuade my husband to think his girl not so bad as he fancies, for he not only *damp* her spirits but ours." "So he *do* mamma," said Miss Lydia, breaking through the stupid vacuity of her countenance with a vivacity that surprised me. "Caroline can't be so veak as papa *think*, or she could not have gone so much in the phaeton, when she knew I hated to ride 'stuffed' up in the coach." "Hold your tongue, child!" said the father gravely; "you know the phaeton was ordered for your sister's *use*, not your *whims*." She was silenced and looked sullen. Pitying the poor girl at my side, who had shown unequivocal marks of *feeling*, as well as of *impatience*, I proposed to her to withdraw into my apartment, and Miss Leonora followed me with alacrity. She immediately went to the harp, and with a touch convinced me that she was no mean proficient on the instrument, any more than in singing, though she pleaded being out of practice, since she had left her school. Sir Murdoch, attracted by our voices from the garden, craved admittance for himself and Mr. Serge, pleading that the other ladies had left him to visit the invalid. Mr. Serge with much apparent curiosity examined the room and me by turns; and at length he said, "Pray, young lady, what is the name of the boarding-school where you were trained?" I replied that I had never been in any school, having had the good fortune of living with a lady who instructed me herself. "There is nothing like it," said he, nodding his head sagaciously. "*My Caroline* was educated at home by a good aunt, and though she cannot draw, nor play, as you and Nora do, yet she is a very sensible and good young woman, and I think you will like her." I told him, I had postponed my own gratification, lest my visit should be troublesome, till she had somewhat recovered from the effects of her journey. "Ah, poor thing!" said he with emotion, "there is the rub! she is too good for this world! But you will say, when you know her, that you never saw a more patient sufferer!"

In a word, it appears to me, that poor Mr. Serge can talk of nothing but his daughter: that his lady can do any thing better than command her tongue: that Miss Lydia is an automaton, useful to fetch and carry; and that the beauty is neither in her element here, nor contented any where. So much for my first four-and-twenty hours knowledge of this illustrious family.

Good Night!

LETTER XL

From the same to the same.

I suppose I shall have no intelligence of our friends at Hartley-pool, more direct than what Mary sends me from Heathcot. Malcolm is not in spirits, he confesses that he never had a more difficult lesson to practise, than the one at present assigned him, which is to amuse Mr. Serge at Tarefield, instead of guarding the Hesperian fruit at Heartley-pool. He told me this morning with a very solemn countenance, that he heard Alice's beauty had gained her the first post of honour, and that she was much admired. I laughed him out of his folly; but it may not be amiss for Mary to give Alice a hint not to look *too handsome* at Heartley-pool.

Miss Serge's increased indisposition has prevented my visiting her till this morning; Doctor Douglass was consulted, and he has happily succeeded in relieving the pain she suffered. On congratulating her mother, she replied, "to be sure, it is a comfort to see her *heasy*: but, dear me! the thing is to see it last." And with this observation she seemed to have dismissed the subject of her daughter's indisposition, and she talked only of the *lakes*, and her surprise that she had lived so many years in the world without having heard of them till within a few months.

The fond father, in the mean time, now looks up to the doctor with the most sanguine hopes; and is as completely domesticated here as if he had been born at the Hall. Malcolm is the delight of his eyes, and Mr. and Mrs. Wilson are, in his own words, "extraordinary people." We contrive by their aid to amuse him many hours in the day; and the good baronet has not been interrupted in his pursuits: he appears to enjoy the enlargement of the circle, particularly in the evening. Last night, after supper, Mr. Serge could talk of nothing but his day's amusement. He had been with his friends and guides to see Wereland Place, a farm in speculation, as you know, for Malcolm. "It is very odd," observed he, "that when I lived in London and kept tight to the *board*, as I may say, I used to think of the pleasure, I should enjoy in the country; but when there, I was always weary of walking about before sunset. Now I think this was because I had nothing to do but to walk about, and that it was idleness, not the country, of which I was tired. Pray how old is Mr. Wilson?" Malcolm thought he was turned of fifty. "Surprising!" observed Mr. Serge; "what a colour, and what activity! There is nothing like the life of a farmer! I have given Mr. Wilson a hint to-day that I should like to purchase something in this neighbourhood. I should not cavil at any price, that would fix me upon you, my young friend, as an apprentice in the farming business. I see clearly that in order to enjoy the country, a man must have country business on his hands: you would, I dare say, help a young beginner to know oats from barley." He shook Malcolm's hand with cordiality, and added in a low voice something at which he laughed heartily, and which produced a crimson blush in Malcolm's face. "How would Mrs. Serge and the young ladies like to give up the fashionable world, for the business of the dairy and the retirement of the country?" asked he. "Dear me!" answered Mrs. Serge, "I *ham* so used to Mr. Serge's *vays* that he know I only laugh at his *vims*. I am sure he is tired to death at Putney, if he stay with us a week at a time! He would make a fine hand of it, to live in this part of the world, where *vone* do not see a soul by the week together!" "Are there any noblemen's seats near you, Mr. Maclairn?" asked Miss Leonora, checking her mother's loquacity. "Not many," was the answer. "So much the better," replied Mr. Serge, "I never courted their custom nor their acquaintance: let every man keep his station and place, and 'cut his coat according to his cloth,' in more ways than one. I am a man who love proper subordination, though I hate slavery. An army is badly disciplined, in my mind, when the commanding officers are 'hail fellow well met' with the privates; and when I see a lord or a duke quit his rank, I understand how matters are going on. I have not lived in the world for nothing." "Well but, papa," said the lively Miss Nora, seizing in a moment her father's allusion, "I suppose there is no sin in a private soldier's rising in his regiment if he can do so honourably." "Certainly not, child," answered Mr. Serge. "Why then do you persist in refusing the borough offered you, and being knighted? Your family might be the better for good connections, sir, and yourself more useful, than in your present private station." "You talk, Nora, like a girl," answered the placid father; "but all the world knows, child, though it has not yet reached you, that the borough and the title, might have been purchased by any man as well as your father; I neither liked the price, nor the duty; and I trust, those who had the bargain, will like it better than I did mine for clothing the army," added he, turning to Sir Murdoch. "It requires a better head than I have," pursued he, "to make contracts with the present managers. I give you my word they understand very well how to make a good bargain for the public purse; and I found their *shears* cut closer than *mine*, notwithstanding my experience in the use of them. However, it is all well: I am quit, with knowing I never spoiled a poor fellow's clothing of a year, for the sake of cabbaging a shilling's worth of the stuff." He laughed heartily at this specimen of his wit, and enjoyed ours with delight. These Serges, Lucy: amuse me, they exhibit to me characters, which, if not singular in themselves, are new to me. My standard for human nature, and human conduct, requires some medium: as it stood at Heathcot, it was too much elevated for the multitude; and in my respect for virtue, you have often reproached me, for wanting pity for folly. I am persuaded that you would at present be satisfied with me. I am neither tempted to laugh, nor to yawn, when Mrs. Serge, in all the simplicity of kindness, pities my *dull life,* and promises me to exact from Sir Murdoch and Lady Maclairn a positive engagement to send me to her in the winter months. "Though Putney is not St. James's-street," adds she, "I so manage, that it is always next door to any public amusements I like: and as Leonora will expect to see Lunnun next winter, as a young woman, you may be sure of my not being a *'house dove.'* To say the truth," continued she, "I think people gain nothing by giving up the pleasures of youth, supposing always they are innocent. Who would believe Lady Maclairn, for example, was not much more than three years older than I; and when I try to recall her beauty and cheerful temper to my memory as they struck me when I first knew her, I can hardly believe she is the Harriet Flamall every body was in love with. To be sure youth *have* its hour, but cheerfulness will last to all seasons, if people do not starve it out by indolence. However," added she, "poor Harriet *have* had trials I never had; and between ourselves, I have heard my aunt Priscilla say, that she was early in life doomed to sorrow, from the death of a young man she loved." We have had many such conversations as these in our walks; for I devote my mornings to Lady Maclairn's service. Mrs. Serge is delighted with Mrs. Wilson, and no less pleased with my friends at the cottages, to whom she has been liberal in her donations. But with all my labours I can perceive that she is heartily tired of being at Tarefield; and yesterday she consulted me very gravely on the propriety of requesting that Caroline might remain at the Hall during her excursion to the lakes. "I have no doubt," added she with alacrity and contentment, "of Mr. Serge's preferring to stay with Caroline. Lydia shall remain also, to amuse her; and Mr. Maclairn will not refuse to squire us. The coach will just hold us, and we shall have a charming *frolic*!" For a moment I felt angry, but the innocence of heart, which is the companion of this weak head, softened me. I with all gentleness, therefore, hinted at the appearance of unkindness and indifference which the proposal of itself would convey to the mind of her daughter; and withal asserted, that I knew Mr. Maclairn had engagements, which would prevent his leaving Tarefield for any time. "That is unlucky," replied she; "and since matters do not favour our scheme it may be as well to say nothing about it. I should have liked to give you *a frolic*; I am sure you have not too much pleasure here; but trust to me for next winter: you shall see Lunnun, if it cost me a journey for myself to fetch you. I have not forgot my young days yet, nor what young folks like." I could not be angry, Lucy. I *answered* her *intention*, and thanked her for her kindness, telling her also very civilly, that I had been frequently months at a time in London during the winter, but that I had never regretted the absence of London amusements at Tarefield. She lifted up her hands and eyes, and said I amazed her. I quitted her during her surprise, saying I was going to sit with Miss Serge an hour.

In continuation.—I am just returned from visiting the poor declining Caroline. She is a modest unaffected young woman, and resembles her youngest sister. I think her features are still more regular than hers, and her large black eyes more expressive, from the languor of sickness that softens down their jetty lustre. I fancy too she is naturally fairer than Leonora, at least her paleness indicates a clearer complexion. She is extremely defective in her shape: I do not recollect having seen a person more crooked; and I cannot help thinking the dreadful spasms in her stomach have originated in the distortion of her shape, and from the compression it is doomed to suffer. She was in her easy chair, and the emblem of neatness: the room in exact order, and at her hand a book. I congratulated her on her exemption from pain, and told her that our favourite, Doctor Douglass, was in danger of being spoiled by our gratitude for having relieved her. She meekly bowed, and, thanking me, spoke of Lady Maclairn's kindness, and the fatigue she had so unfortunately introduced. "I was entirely governed by my wishes to oblige my parents," added she, "in hazarding a journey; being convinced that I can expect no benefit to accrue to me from leaving Putney. But it amuses my family, and diverts my dear father's thoughts from an event which he considers with too much tenderness and grief. I am pleased by Doctor Douglass's frankness," continued she; "he honestly owns, that he sees no advantage for me in travelling; and he has contrived to convince my friends that I cannot be better than *at home*. They do not understand him; *but I do*, Miss Cowley." You will suppose my reply. "You read sometimes, I see," said I, taking up the volume on the table: it was the Economy of Human Life. "My little library contains some authors who will not disgrace yours. I will bring the catalogue." "Your recommendation of one will suffice," answered she, pensively smiling, "for I am not able to read much. My father reads frequently to me; and if you will favour me with any periodical work I shall be obliged to you; he is fond of works of that sort." I promised to send the "Mirror" to her room, she not having read it; and I quitted her in a proper frame of mind to visit Miss Flint. She appears to me to be considerably mended in her health, and she was more cheerful than I have seen her for a long time. I always thought solitude a good remedy for those who could not enjoy society, or rather who spoiled it. She was chatty, and of course I was not ill humoured. She asked me many questions relative to our guests; and particularly whether the "table was abundant and handsome." "I hope it is so," added she; "for I was explicit with Harriet on that point. Her friends' entertainment I shall consider as my concern; under this roof it ought to be so." "I only wish you could contrive to share in your hospitality below stairs," observed I, "I am certain it might be effected without pain to you, or trouble to the servants, more than one five minutes would accomplish." She shook her head, and said she was fearful of breaking into the regimen which the doctor had prescribed, and from which she trusted for some relief; and that since Mrs. Allen had so kindly devoted her time to her, she had all the comfort her situation needed. "However," added she, "I should be vexed if these good people fancied I shunned them from pride; and I think I am equal to receiving them as tea-visitors; will you propose it to them, when you think the gentlemen will be absent." "Let it be this evening then," replied I with gaiety: "you will find that company will not lessen your hopes from an abstemious diet." She consented, and I left her to announce my commission.

In continuation.—Wednesday morning. We assembled yesterday in Miss Flint's stale apartment: even the poor Caroline was of the party. The first *coup d'œil* convinced me that Miss Flint had not quite done with this vain world: all was in state; and the heiress of Tarefield, in a fine muslin wrapping gown trimmed with lace, received us with much ceremony, but with no want of kindness. Lady Maclairn officiated at the tea-table; and Mrs. Serge, whose attention had been much engaged with the various decorations of the room, now suddenly surveying the ponderous *silver* tea-board and tea-kettle, *wondered*, according to custom, that her ladyship did not exchange that heavy old fashioned plate for what was tasty and "*helegant.*" Miss Flint, with a spice of her ancient asperity, observed, that it had been long in the Flint family, and she preferred it to more modern. "I beg your pardon," replied the unconscious offender, "I did not know it belonged to you, madam; but I cannot unsay what I have said. I know some folks think old-fashioned plate honourable to themselves, as it proves their family's opulence; but for my part, it is not my notion that honour depend upon any such things. I lately sold a silver bowl which held three gallons, that had been my great-grandfather's. You Lady Maclairn," added she, laughing, "being of the Hatchway family: you will, perhaps, blame me; for it was an *onourable* bowl, as I can affirm. It was a present from the ship's *howners*, for his fighting with a privateer and sinking her: the whole story was engraved on the *rim*, with the names of the '*howners,*' and of the ship my great grandfather saved from the enemy." "I certainly should have preserved it," replied Lady Maclairn, "as an evidence so honourable to the captain's bravery, and his employers' gratitude." "Dear me!" answered she, "who trouble themselves with things of this sort after they are past away a little while! It was quite useless to me, so I exchanged it for a "*hapron*" and some egg-cups, with other trifles." The saucy Leonora laughed immoderately. "You ought to say, my dear madam, an *eparne.*" Without a muscle of my face being moved, "I beg your pardon," said I, "but as the word is a French one, a stranger to the language may excuse the liberty of being corrected in the pronouncing it. *Epargner*, means to save, or to spare, and this elegant ornament for a table is not misnamed; for it is commonly filled with trifles which cost but little to the donor of a feast." "Thank you, my dear Miss Cowley," said she, with perfect good humour, "you have taught me what I did not know before; and if Nora had employed her knowledge of the French tongue as well, she would not have disgraced her *heducation*, by laughing at her mother." Leonora blushed, and answered that she had called it an *epargne* constantly in her hearing, but thought she might be deemed *impertinent* to carry her "*critique*" farther.

"Rather say, child," replied the good-natured mother, "that you did not wish me to understand *heparner* was *to save*, lest, like your Lady Gudgeon, I should grudge you clean gloves, and fill, as she *do*, my *heparner* with wax oranges and apples." It was now her turn to laugh, and we gave no offence by joining in her mirth. A rubber of *"Vhisk"* completed the evening; and Miss Flint, graciously thanking her for her company, saw us depart without any signs of being fatigued by her exertions.

Next Tuesday we are to go to Durham to pass the day. Mrs. Serge has wisely given up the project of seeing the lakes; and as something must be done to please her, Lady Maclairn has promised to accompany her in this jaunt. If you are not grateful, so much the worse; for not only *time*, but labour is lost to

Your

Rachel Cowley.

LETTER XLII

From the same to the same.

Our good doctor will have a more rich and costly offering from the grateful Mr. Serge, than any that ostentation or superstition ever gave to Esculapius, or to any saint in the Roman calendar, if he can manage to keep his patient as many years as he has done hours from the cruel invader, pain. Yet I am angry with Douglass's honesty; he tells me that this poor girl cannot live long; and that even the medicine we fancy so efficacious, will soon lose its benign effect. "She knows her condition," added he with sympathy, "and has only the wish of seeing her father more reconciled to the thoughts of losing her; but we must let him enjoy the present, and trust for the future to that Being who will support him."

The day before yesterday, Miss Leonora and myself went to Bishop's Auckland for an airing. The dapper Mr. William Willet, Mr. Serge's servant, attended us: and I, very successfully, conducted the whisky to Mrs. Crofts' door. The good old lady received us with great kindness; and after making a few purchases, her daughter attended us to the circulating library, the principal object with Miss Nora. We found this shop was in the same street with Susan Crofts', and its rival for smartness. My companion, who had languished for *books* at the Hall, instantly proceeded to make an ample selection. Scores were produced *that had been read*—a *score at least* put aside for her use; and I thought our business finished here, when Miss Leonora accidentally took up a new novel which "she had been *dying* to see for a month;" but the third volume was in circulation: it was hourly expected, however, and the shopman would send it with the fourth and last. This civility would not do. The young lady could not wait: she would purchase the work rather than not have it: she should be quite miserable not to take it home with her, her curiosity having been excited by seeing it within her reach. "Has any of your neighbours this book, Mr. Type?" asked Miss Crofts; "perhaps, by sending, you might get the volume for the young lady." "He would endeavour: a gentleman at the Mitre had hired it the preceding day, and perhaps he had done with it." He alertly stepped to the door to cross to the inn, when, as quickly returning to make way for the envied possessor of the third volume, he began to urge his request, and the young lady's wishes for the complete set of the work. A graceful compliance followed from a very handsome man of about thirty; and who, addressing me, very gallantly declared that "he was *inexpressibly flattered* in contributing in the smallest degree to *Miss Cowley*'s wishes and pleasure." *Miss Cowley*, who saw no necessity for incurring an obligation where the obliger had so manifest an advantage over her, in regard to his knowledge of her name, only coldly bowed, and said that not having any peculiar interest to gratify by his politeness, she would refer him to her young friend for those thanks due for his indulgence of her curiosity. "*I* am indeed, sir," said Miss Serge, "extremely obliged to you; but I shall not long detain the work, for I read very quick. *To-morrow evening* they will be returned, or the next morning at *furthest*." He bowed, and we left the shop, ordering the books to Susan Crofts'. In our way I asked Susan the name of this civil gentleman who had been so ready to contribute to "Miss Cowley's" happiness. "He was a stranger, lately come to Bishop's Aukland. He lodged at the Mitre Inn, she believed, for she had seen him there several times within a day or two, and she thought him a very handsome man." "I think he has a very good person," replied I. "He thinks so himself, I am certain," observed Miss Nora, "by the elaborate pains he takes to display it." I made no answer, for I perceived that gratitude had not banished the young lady's displeasure, in having been overlooked for the gentleman's "Miss Cowley." Mrs. Crofts in our absence had sent for my frost-bitten friends from their school, and had set out her cake and wine, whilst Willet was stowing the cargo of books in the vehicle, and waiting with it at the door. My greetings with the children detained me some little time: I did not perceive even that my companion had quitted the parlour till I rose to depart; but concluded, when I did miss her, that she was in the shop. I was mistaken, she was not there; but approaching the door, expecting to find her by the carriage, I saw her coming from Mr. Type's with hasty steps. On expressing my surprise at her absence, she told me that she had fortunately discovered, in taking out her purse to pay Miss Crofts, that she had left her pocketbook on the bookseller's counter, "and judging it the securest method, I went for it myself," added she; "luckily I found it, exactly as I supposed, concealed by the books I had rejected. Only think! That coxcomb was still in the shop. How fortunate that he did not see it!" I smiled, for I saw through this little coquetry. "It would not have been pleasant to me, I do assure you," pursued she, "to have seen it in his hands; for one does not write one's thoughts for every eye. Neither do I believe it would have pleased Mr. Malcolm to have seen this beau at the Hall on the pretence of giving *you* your strayed goods." — "I do not see the drift of your inference," replied I; "for what concern could Mr. Maclairn have had in a business so exclusively yours? However, I am glad you have recovered your book, and spared the gentleman the trouble of a visit to the Hall." — "We might, notwithstanding, have made such a visit a diversion for ourselves," answered she with gaiety; "for, to speak the truth, I think your lover would not be the worse for a little jealousy. He is too secure; and wants the hopes and anxieties of *la belle passion* to rouse him: You really are as dull as though brother and sister. I cannot conceive how you contrive to keep up your cheerfulness at Tarefield: what with your *prudent lover*, and the sober routine at the Hall, I think you as much to be pitied as I am." "Much the same," answered I, laughing; "for my calamities are as imaginary as your own. I love the country, and the retirement at the Hall; and I am attached to its inmates. I am so completely Malcolm Maclairn's *sister* that I am his chief confident, and he reads his love letters to me. He will soon, I trust, be married to a very amiable, deserving young lady, to whom he has been attached several years: she resides with her mother in this neighboured; but she is at present from home." "Good heavens!" exclaimed Miss Nora with a pretty theatrical air, "you make me envy this Phillis! With such a swain as Mr. Maclairn, and with a mind suitable to her situation in life, and the society in which she will probably pass all her days, how happy is her condition when compared with mine!" "Miss Heartley," replied I, "has been educated by a mother who has prepared her to act properly in every society and situation in life. Mrs. Heartley has lived in the world, and is a superior woman." "My lot, then," said she, "is misery to this young lady's!" She spoke with emotion. "Do not answer me," continued she, "till you have reflected on my reasons for discontent. With an education which has taught me to blush at ignorance, and to be offended by vulgarity; accustomed to enjoy with girls of fashion, rank, and fortune, the advantages and the hopes which have resulted from my situation with them; I am now doomed to live in a society, in which I am hourly exposed to give offence and to be offended. Be ingenuous, my dear Miss Cowley! Tell me, do you think that seven years and more passed in one of the first schools in town, can have rendered me a fit inmate for my father's house, or a suitable companion for my mother's acquaintance? I read in your countenance that my appeal has reached your heart. Can you be surprised that I am disgusted and repining in parties composed of shopkeepers and their wives, masters of ships, and genteel people who, in my mother's dialect, live "right up," viz. on their little fortune, and who, fancying they are *gentry*, because they have no longer the drudgery of opening a shop and standing behind its counter, affect airs truly ridiculous, and even sickening to me. It was entirely owing to Caroline's influence with my father that we came hither, instead of being dragged down to Y—m—th with a party of my mother's "*hold*" friends, Mr. Crimp the coal merchant and his family; and it was not without some difficulty that we prevailed on my mother to give up the *tower* of Norfolk which these her *hold* friends had proposed. But I would have died sooner than have submitted! I have met with mortifications at Bath, which will prevent my having the folly of ever being seen again in a place of public resort without proper introduction! This was a fear I never experienced at school, when looking forwards to my freedom from its confinement. *Miss Serge*, the contracter's daughter, was there on a level with the first girls in the house; nor was there one pupil in it whose masters were more liberally paid, for my mother chose I should make them presents every vacation; and she was equally attentive to secure me favour with the governess and teachers. Amongst the girls to whom I was particularly attached were the two Miss Gudgeons. Their father Sir Ambrose was dead; and their mother, Lady Gudgeon, lived too gay a life to think much of their comforts or wants. Almira Gudgeon confided to me her discontents and difficulties; and in return she shared my purse. It grieved me to leave her at school during the holidays; and on my mentioning to my father and mother those neglected girls, they invited them to Putney the following vacation. Lady Gudgeon made no objection; and from that time my friends always accompanied me home. Last midsummer they were removed from school, and sent down to their mother's house in Berkshire. From this place I received poor Almira's melancholy letters: though then turned of seventeen, she lived immured at the Dale with no other company than that of her sister, an old nurse, and the gardener's family. The winter approached, and I had the pleasure of hearing that my beloved Almira and her sister would be *brought out* at Bath, as soon as the Birth Day was over. Lady Gudgeon having been with them for a week, and finding Clara in danger of growing too fat, had engaged to introduce her with her sister, on condition that she left off suppers and took more exercise. You may judge of the joy I felt on gaining my mother's promise of taking me to Bath; and the still greater satisfaction I had on finding that Lydia was included in the family party, instead of being left with me at Mrs. S——'s, as preparatory to reconciling her to the confinement and instruction she was thought to want. I had foreseen the ridicule I must have braved; and with a heart exulting at this escape, and palpitating with expected pleasure, and the hope of meeting my friends, we reached Bath, and settled ourselves on the South Parade.

"In a few days after our arrival Lady Gudgeon's name appeared on the list of new comers, and my joy was complete. Her ladyship's condescension enchanted my mother; and kind hearted as she is, the Miss Gudgeons constantly received from her hands tickets for the play, and their mother found a carriage at her command. During the space of three weeks, or a month, we constantly made one party. I saw my mother nightly paying for her lessons at Lady Gudgeon's *vingt-et-une* table; but of what importance was a little money to my father? Yet he appeared every day to like the Gudgeons less and less; and at length forbad my mother's playing cards at the Rooms with her ladyship, or going to her parties at home. On some occasions it is in vain to reason with my father. My mother submitted, and I was told that my young friends were silly, giddy girls, who did me no good. I perfectly understood that my father had judged with precision on Clara Gudgeon's character; for I knew she was deceitful and selfish, and she had shown herself to me in her true colours from the first ball in which I had been noticed for my dancing. I also was no stranger to her malice from the time her favourite Captain Fairly became attentive and polite to me. Caroline's increasing illness at this juncture prevented our amusements, and gave an ostensible reason for my mother's declining Lady Gudgeon's invitations. At length Caroline was better; and my mother joined a family party, who lodged at the next house, and with whom my father was become very sociable. As I had been engaged to dance with Captain Fairly at this ball, I was not willing to be disappointed; and knowing that I should meet the Miss Gudgeons, I meant to join them, when at the Rooms. My mother had already placed herself at a card-table with her new acquaintance when Lady Gudgeon entered the room. Following the example of the young lady, my companion, I kept close by my mother's side, waiting for Captain Fairly's summons. 'How is this, my dear Mrs. Serge?' cried Lady Gudgeon, advancing towards her with a smile; 'you here! and a deserter! But you will find your place, when your rubber is up.'—'I thank your ladyship,' replied my unembarrassed mother, 'but, to tell you the truth, I do not like your game so well as *vhist*, for I do not so well understand it.' A stifled titter from the surrounding groupe followed this speech. 'As you please, Mrs. Serge,' answered her ladyship, moving on without deigning to notice me, or the smile of contempt from those she passed. She took her post, opened the cards, and sent for her daughters. They had, I presume, their instructions; for in passing me they did not see me, and in repassing me I was saluted with a broad stare and a giggle, which I had seen too often practised not to comprehend. I was prepared for the neglect I met with in the dance. The Miss Gudgeons neither spoke nor deigned to turn hands with me, and whilst their heads were adorned with feathers and turbands of my giving, their looks of scorn cut me to the soul. Captain Fairly saw my distress, and their rudeness; and said something to Clara on her carelessness in the dance. With an insolent laugh she asked him whether his credit was out with his old taylor, that he so diligently courted a new one. This was too much for me to bear, and I gave up dancing for the remainder of the evening. But my mortifications were not yet finished. After having heard my mother announce that arts were trumps, seen her mark her *onours*, and win the rubber, although she had the curse of Scotland every time in her *and*, the party broke up, and the lady proposed going into the ball room to give her daughter a caution to dance no more. On entering it I was astonished to see my good father quietly standing, with his two thumbs hooked under each arm, and enjoying the sight of the dancers. He expressed his surprise at finding me idle, and said he had come on purpose to see me dance, having left Caroline *purely*. Fairly urged me to go down the dance then commencing, and encouraged by him, I was determined to show my spirit. In our way we encountered Miss Clara Gudgeon. 'By your leave, fair lady,' cried my father, bustling through the groupe. 'Bless me!' said Miss Clara, 'is it you Mr. Serge? Are you come to see fashions?'—'Even so,' replied he, 'but if you are of my mind you will think those at Putney as good as any here, and, for ought I can see, you footed it away in my parlour with ten couple as merrily as you do here. But where is Almira? I hope she has her Putney holiday face; for yours seems as clouded as when your six weeks' gambols finished with us.' 'I really cannot direct you, sir,' answered she, retreating; 'but if you cannot see *her*, she will undoubtedly soon perceive you.' A loud laugh, and a disdainful toss of her head accompanied this speech; but my father, not conceiving that her intention could be uncivil, went on searching for Almira, till I told him that they had been offended by my mother's not joining her ladyship's party. He only nodded, and said it was all very well. From this time the Gudgeons were strangers to us; and because Captain Fairly chose to be civil they *cut him*. He laughed at their impertinence; but I had no pleasure at Bath after this, as you may imagine."

In my animadversions on Miss Leonora's little narrative you will not suspect me of sparing the Gudgeon family; and I added, that neither the simplicity of her father, nor her mother's provincial dialect would stand in her way with the discriminating and the virtuous. "It is easy to think, and to say this," replied she with vivacity, "when we are remote from the regrets and dissatisfactions of living with those who can neither guide nor improve us: who do not even know when they wound, nor can comprehend why they offend. If I sing I am asked whether it be a psalm or song, and they wish for Alley Croaker, God save the King, or Black-eyed Susan. If I play, it must be Handel's Water Piece or the Variations of Nancy Dawson. Oh! you know not the misery," added she, bursting into tears, "of being doomed to live with those who are perpetually disgusting our taste, opposing our feelings, and contradicting by their habits and modes of life those which more refinement have rendered necessary and essential to our comfort! Indeed, Miss Cowley, I speak from bitter experience; and I sometimes wish that, like Lydia, I had been kept at home, and been happy in ignorance." I was struck by her acuteness, and moved by her distress; and with much seriousness I exhorted her to correct a sensibility which tended more to cherish a fastidious refinement of feeling, than a love for what was commendable. "Believe me, my dear young friend," added I, "that although not educated as a girl at a fashionable boarding school, nor in Lady Gudgeon's societies, your father's character has been perfectly understood by me, you will find in him your pride and boast, by weighing his trifling defects with his integrity and uprightness of heart." "I know his worth," replied she, weeping, "he must be loved; but what will you say for my mother?"—"What I really think," replied I, "and must ever think, till I find out, that a little knowledge is judged to be an equivalent for a base mind. I would rather, a thousand times over, be Mrs. Serge's child than Lady Gudgeon's; and I would convince the world by my respect to such a parent that I was qualified to appreciate what was really estimable in it; and by my resentment check the idle laugh of those, more incorrigible in their ignorance than the object they contemned: for it must be allowed, at least, that Mrs. Serge is not *conceited*. Your education has been liberal," continued I; "you have endowments which your mother has not; and for a plain reason, she had not the means of acquiring them. Show your parents that their kindness has not been thrown away; and above all things manifest to others that you are superior to the ingratitude and meanness of despising your benefactors, because they happen to be less fashionable than yourself in the cut of their garment or in their address."

We now entered the avenue, and Leonora composed her pretty face, saying, with a deep sigh, that she wanted a true friend! I silently agreed with her. I leave to Mary the profound reflections which this little airing has brought forward in my mind; it not being my business to reason, but to detail. Heathcot and its inhabitants must not engage me a moment longer; for I am Lady Maclairn's "right hand."

Yours ever,

Rachel Cowley.

P. S. Mrs. Allen sends you her blessing. She is Miss Flint's *right hand*, and comforter to boot: but when, and where is it that she fails in goodness?

LETTER XLIII

From the same to the same.

Saturday evening.

A deluge of rain has fallen here since last night; of course we have all been stationary to-day. My spirits rose, however, before dinner on seeing our doctor enter in his oiled surtout, like a river god, dispensing his streams every step he made towards us. I escaped a shower-bath by my flight; and leaving Miss Nora to her heroes and heroines, I took my netting-box, determining to pass an hour with Miss Serge. She was pleased, and moreover she was cheerful. In less than ten minutes we were interrupted by Miss Lydia, who, with blubbered cheeks, and much anger, threw a muslin robe on the bed; and showing us a quantity of fine narrow lace, which she held in her hand, said, with renewed tears, "Is it not a 'burning shame' that I am to be always the drudge to Nora? Why ca'nt she do her own jobs? She can move her fingers fast enough when she *like* at her music; a thimble would do them no more harm than her harp strings. I will tell my father how I am *put upon* by her: that I will!" "My dear Lydia," said the gentle Caroline, "I will help you. Willet has a great deal to do, or she should take it: but it is a trifle, and I am certain you would not vex your father for a trifle." "You always talk in *that there* way," replied Lydia, wiping her eyes, and visibly softened; "but I promise you, *you* shall not have any thing to do with this gown. We had enough of your helping to prepare Nora's two dresses a day, at Bath. Such learning say I! She ought to be ashamed of herself! To see a sick sister work for her, and one older than herself made her waiting-woman." She proceeded to the performance of her allotted task without further delay; and I perceived that she had dexterity at her needle. "I will read you a pretty story from the Mirror," said I, taking up the book, "that will amuse you, Miss Lydia." "I am much obliged to you," replied she; "but if you will read from this book I shall like it better." Thus saying, she drew from her pocket a dirty, mutilated book, intitled "Joe Miller's Jests." Caroline's black eyes wanted not spirit, when with resentment and vexation she asked where she had picked up such trash. "Trash!" repeated Lydia, "I do not know what you mean by trash! It will not make you cry, as that book *have* done. I am sure, when we read this, we laughed till our sides ached." "*We!*" echoed Caroline, "who do you mean?" "Why Willet, and Mrs. Patty, and ——," she hesitated,—"and Mr. William." "Why will you thus grieve me, Lydia? Why will you thus force me to grieve your dear father," said Caroline, "do you not know that he is displeased when you seek your society in the servants' hall? Did William give you that book?" "Lord! no," answered Miss Lydia with terror. "I found it in Jacob's coat pocket, he only read *here* and *there* a bit." "And did you not blush, Lydia, when you produced a book purloined from a postillion's pocket, which a better informed servant saw was not proper for him to read to females, even of his own class?" "How should I know that?" replied she. "You know, I suppose, that you have been forbidden to talk with your father's postillions, to frequent the kitchen, or to take the lead in the servants'-hall. Willet also knows my father's commands; but enough of this: I shall inform him they are disobeyed." Miss Lydia burst into tears, and, imploring her sister to say nothing of this matter, she faithfully promised to restore the book to its owner by means of the cook maid, and never to go near the servants'-hall again. This contest had too much fretted poor Caroline. I saw that she was again in pain, and pretending to more industry than I had, I helped Lydia to finish the trimming business; leaving the invalid to recover her tranquillity. The poor girl amazed at my condescension, asked whether I did all my own *jobs*; for she concluded that Miss Cowley had been at a London boarding school, because she played on the harp.

Tell me in your next that you have had enough of my talents in the gossiping way. I have only to fear that Horace will suspect my understanding is in its retrograde motion, for I have not written to him this last fortnight a letter which would not disgrace a Miss in her Teens. "Evil communications corrupt good manners." This is not my apology: but folly is catching, and you have betrayed me into such an observance of it, that I yesterday, without reflection, began a speech with "all *mander* of persons." So look to the consequences of my readiness to assume any form or language, my Lucy prescribes for her

Faithful,

Rachel Cowley.

In continuation.—I am inclined to believe that Miss Leonora is emulous of rivaling her grandmamma, Mrs. Hatchway, in her hairbreadth escapes by sea and land. Whilst I thought her shut up in her room, and *devouring* Monimia, the heroine of a good novel intitled the Manor-House, she was in the avenue enjoying a shower-bath. In returning, completely drenched, her mother perceived her from the window, and as I conceived, unseasonably stopped her in her way to dry her clothes, by an angry lecture on her folly and heedlessness. "I am not surprised," added she, in a sharp tone, "that I cannot keep a laundry-maid: six or eight white dresses in a week to wash would tire any one's patience."

It is probable the lecture would have concluded with this notable observation, had not Mrs. Serge unluckily perceived at this instant the lamentable breach which the brambles had made in the costly deep lace which trimmed Miss Leonora's pelisse. "I don't believe," exclaimed she, surveying the mischief, "there is on the face of the whole earth your *hequal*, Nora! Your hextravagance is enough to discredit a polite *heducation*! Though your father is a rich man he has something better to do with his money than to buy you every month a twenty guinea lace. Here's a sight! It would provoke a saint! One would think you had not *common sense* to walk in the pouring rain, and through *edges* and ditches with a new thirty-pound *pelisse*." Miss Nora laughed, not without contempt. "Never mind," said she, rudely, snatching the tattered and wet pelisse from her mother's hand, "it is only another evidence that the Serges with all their wealth are too poor for the purchase of common sense, or good manners:" then, with a curtsey to Lady Maclairn, she retired to change her dress. Mrs. Serge, with an heightened colour following her steps. I believe this *brouillerie* became more serious in their apartment. The young lady did not appear at the dining table, and Mrs. Serge's fair face still glowed. "Where is Nora?" asked the father, adjusting his napkin under his chin. "Does she dine with Caroline?" "No," replied the wife, "she is busy drying the books Sam has brought her from the library, they are as wet as water can make them, and she has had enough of the rain for one day." Her folly was related with some asperity, and the postillion's drenched condition described. Mr. Serge wished that neither had taken cold; and with a placid air took his soup. When the heroine appeared, she was in perfect good humour; but I perceived that she had been weeping, and look fatigued; something of a deprecating tone and pensive air soon produced their effect on the relenting mother, and all was harmony in the evening. I chanced to ask her what new novels had been sent her from the library. "I have not examined the parcel," replied she with some emotion, "for I have for once discovered that there are certain frames of mind in which a novel cannot be read with either amusement or interest: besides," added she, "I have been teazed with a pain in my teeth, which will be attributed to my morning ramble, notwithstanding I have felt it more than a week:" then turning to Malcolm, with more coquetry than I had ever observed in her manner, she with a sweet smile asked him to prescribe for her; and directed his attention to a tooth as the one which she suspected was diseased. I could not preserve my gravity on seeing the *sang froid* with which Malcolm examined the most beautiful mouth nature could form, and the delight which Mr. Serge manifested at his Nora's choice of a doctor; who with the solemnity of an old nurse acquitted the spotless tooth, and ordered some whey on going to bed.

"It is ten to one," observed Mrs. Serge with good humour, "whether even your remedy, *doctor*, will remove her cold in one night: it will not surprise me that she is laid up for a week." "Why will you anticipate disappointment for her?" asked Mr. Serge, "it will be sufficient when it arrives, and if she cannot see Durham to-morrow, she must take the punishment of her heedlessness; but I warrant the tooth will be well with a good night's sleep." — "I had settled with Caroline, before my offence of the morning had made the excursion to Durham a doubt," answered Leonora, "to remain with her, thinking my sister Lydia would be amused by the jaunt; and to be honest, I confess I have no hope of being quit of a cold that I am sensible is the effect of my indiscretion." "Yes," observed Miss Lydia, "it was settled I should go last Monday, but you know, Nora, you promised to contrive that I should ride in the phaeton, and I would rather stay at home than go in the coach. I am always so deadly sick in a coach, that I hate them." "Nonsense!" cried the mother, "that is a new fagary. You never complained in a close carriage till the phaeton was bought." "Well, my love," observed the placid Mr. Serge, "but as pleasure is the purposed end of our little journey, why should not Lydia have a share of it unmixed, and as our dear girls have agreed in this business, we will manage so as to please Lydia. You will not refuse your assistance, my dear Malcolm," added he, smiling: "you shall have the daughter instead of the father to conduct." Malcolm accepted of the exchange with good humour; and all were contented.

I have had so much business of late on my hands that I believe I have not mentioned the increasing good understanding which subsists between Malcolm and Mr. Parry, our new curate. He is become a frequent and welcome visitor here, and an acquisition we all enjoy. Malcolm has, I suspect, given him a hint that his present duty requires assistance; and most assuredly he finds in Parry an excellent coadjutor. The baronet enjoys his conversation, and Mr. Serge is no burden to him. I foresee we shall not need Parry for to-morrow's excursion. The rain is now pouring down in torrents, and it is midnight. May Heaven guard your pillow, my Lucy, with its accustomed goodness! Mary shall have my journal of the Durham expedition in due time.

Yours, &c.
Rachel Cowley.

LETTER XLIV

From the same to the same.

The interruption in my usual punctuality, my dear friend, and which has alarmed your too tender fears, induces me to write to you without delay, for the express purpose of assuring you that I am perfectly well; and that in my failure during a few posts nothing has occurred to disturb me beyond the concern I have been under for the happiness of those around me. It is not too much to take for granted that you have long since perceived in Miss Leonora Serge's character and opinions certain indications that will prepare you for the recital of her premeditated, and by this time *successful* journey to Gretna-

Green. But as in your code of laws, and modes of instruction Mary will stand no chance of being an adept in the science of intrigue, duplicity, and cunning, it may not be useless to place before her an example so calculated to impress on her mind the delightful gratifications, enjoyed by the girl of spirit, who prefers running away from the restraints of parental care, giving up all the decencies of her sex and condition, and proclaiming to the world that she is void of feeling and principle, in order to attain the man whom she loves for having betrayed her to scorn and ruin.

As I predicted in my last letter, the weather prevented our going to Durham. Miss Nora's tooth-ach became a sore throat, and a slight fever. She was of course an invalid, and poor Sam, the postillion, had more than one drenching commission. Wednesday we had a sun unclouded; and on Thursday we set out for Durham with a doubtful sky, and an oppressive heat in the air. Miss Lydia, stuffed into her mother's pea green riding dress, took her allotted station in the phaeton with Malcolm, with an alacrity and contentment of heart that paid her good father for the sacrifice of his pleasure. Douglas in the curricle with Sir Murdoch, left us nothing to wish for him. Lady Maclairn, your Rachel, and Mr. and Mrs. Serge, had Mr. Parry for their beau; and I saw with pleasure her ladyship cheerfully sustaining her part in this arduous trial of her strength, in an undertaking so averse to her habits of life. The sun favoured the out-riders till we reached Durham. The delicate Lady Maclairn preferring the office of *Caterer*, to a sultry walk, was fortunately left at the inn to quiet and repose, whilst we sallied forth to see the public places; but I believe that in reaching them we saw all that was worthy of notice in the town; and a burst of thunder, and a black cloud, warned us to return with all speed to the shelter of our inn. Happily for us, a deluge of rain spared our timid friends from the terrors of the thunder storm; and ourselves from the pain of seeing them in hysterics, as well as we from any further exhibition at Durham. A card-table and chess-board, with a sumptuous dinner filled up our *pleasurable* time. But no felicity is permanent! Even a party of pleasure is liable to vexations. Lydia's enjoyment of the dessert was interrupted by an altercation between her father and herself. He insisted on her returning home in the coach, urging the dampness of the evening. Miss Lydia contended that the rain had made the evening fair, and much pleasanter than the morning. Mr. Serge was firm, and the pouting girl was forced to yield to his authority. It would have been as well had the young lady been indulged; for it was proved *demonstratively*, that a close carriage did not agree with Miss Lydia Serge: and although we did not concur with her in calling Mr. Serge 'ill-natured and obstinate,' we could not but allow, that less pertinacity on his part would have been *discreet*, and Mrs. Serge's lecture on *gluttony* as well spared for another time and season.

On the carriage's driving up to the hall-door I was shocked on seeing Mrs. Allen advancing with precipitation to meet us: she was weeping; and in evident distress stopped to speak with Malcolm and Mr. Serge; who in a moment endeavoured to quit the phaeton exclaiming aloud, "She is dead! my child is dead!" and Malcolm, giving the rains to a servant, sprang from the carriage and entered the house. Whilst Mrs. Allen in vain repeated to the poor father, "No, no, my good sir: hear me." You will judge that this consternation was not long to be endured. Malcolm's absence was but momentary. "They are alarmed within," said he aloud; and he added with assumed composure, "Miss Leonora is missing; she is probably sheltered in the neighbourhood. I am going at *Miss Serge's* request to seek her, there having been some blundering as to the road which Miss Leonora indicated on leaving the house for a walk." On saying this, Malcolm leaped into the curricle and disappeared. "I see how it is," observed Mr. Serge, panting for breath, "all is clear! but God is merciful! Let me go to my Caroline, let me see my comfort, my darling, and then I shall be patient." Doctor Douglas prevented him, by arguing the danger of agitating her spirits still more than they had been, and we conducted the trembling father into the diningparlour; Mrs. Allen attending Douglas to Caroline's room. Mrs. Serge had, with the astonishment which the scene had produced, lost, apparently, the use of her tongue and powers of reflection. On reaching the parlour she burst into tears; and with more of resentment than despair, observed, that she was only sorry Mr. Maclairn had so much trouble; for she doubted not but Leonora would be at the Hall as soon as himself. "This is her penitence!" continued she; "because I was angry with her for walking in the rain she has stopped at some house, and is, perhaps, laughing at our fears." "Before you are too sanguine in your hopes, Mrs. Serge," said her husband, with much coldness of manner, "it may not be amiss to know when she left this house; and what grounds those whom she has quitted have for their suspicions." Mrs. Warner was summoned. Her evidence consisted in the following particulars. Miss Nora soon after we had left the Hall changed her dress; for Warner met her in the garden at one o'clock equipped for a journey, and with some surprise observed that if she meant to take an airing she would be disappointed, as Mr. Willet was gone with his sister, for the day, to see the castle, and had taken the only horse and carriage remaining, which was the little market cart. The young lady said that she had only thought of a walk in the avenue; but she believed it would be wiser to stay at home, for there would certainly be a thunder shower. "She sauntered with me into the vestibule," continued Warner, "when seeing your shawl, madam," addressing Mrs. Serge, "which you omitted to take with you for Miss Lydia's use, she wrapped it round her, and said she would venture a little way, for she was half dead for want of exercise; and away she tripped, promising not to lose sight of the cottage on the green, which is not a quarter of a mile from hence, hinting that she had promised the old woman who lives there a trifle for her grandchild. I thought no more of the young lady," continued Warner, "till the storm came on, when Mrs. Allen came to see whether she was with Miss Flint or in her own room; saying that Miss Serge wished for her sister's company, as she was a coward when it thundered. We were sadly perplexed, madam. Having no man-servant, but the gardener and his lad, at hand, and the thunder was dreadful here: so Mrs. Allen, trusting to Miss Nora's promise to me, waited a while, saying she was certain it was better that she should remain sheltered in the cottage than to venture home in such a tempest. The rain soon abated, and we sent the gardener with an umbrella to Dame Bank's. She had not seen the lady. You may judge of our fright! The gardner and his son were sent different ways to no purpose. About two hours since they returned in consequence of news they had picked up at the Ram. A traveller who had entered the house during the storm had seen a lady hastening to a chaise and four that stood on the road to Durham. She was assisted by a gentleman, and rather flew than walked to the carriage. She had something white on her head and shoulders, and the gentleman was in scarlet. Whilst they were talking with Hunt and this stranger, Tom Hunt entered. He had passed the chaise on leaving Durham, and had seen the lady in white, but not her face: she seemed to be sleeping on the gentleman's shoulder. My lady," added Warner, "is sadly ruffled and distressed by this disaster; and if Mrs. Allen had not been with Miss Serge, God knows what would have been the event of a day so dreadful as this has been! My lady and Mrs. Allen only fear they have done wrong, in not sending an express to Durham, as soon as the men returned; but as so much time had been lost, and they hoped you would not be late on the road, they gave up the thought; and, indeed, it was impossible to have gained any advantage from pursuing it." "You say truly, my good woman," observed Mr. Serge, with suppressed agony, "The child who forsakes a parent's protection cannot be benefited by being pursued. But repentance will overtake her. No, she is gone, gone for ever!" added he rising and pacing the room! — Lady Maclairn retired with Warner. Again the poor old man quitted his seat, and deliberately taking off his wig, wiped his head and eyes. "Where is the heart, Miss Cowley," said he, "that would not bleed to see such a girl as my Nora thus lost, thus betrayed to folly and wretchedness? Poor creature!" added he, "how hard is thy fate! A mere babe, as one may say, thus to be ensnared and deluded! Thus to be the victim of designs, which a highway robber would scorn, as beneath him. But to the villain who has robbed me of my child, will I place the pangs I feel; God learnt from that child the knowledge of my sufferings!" He was silent for some time, nor did his lady attempt to comfort him: she appeared stupified by the blow, and I trembled for her safety. On seeing me apply my salts to relieve her, he again rose and said to her, "I pity you; but remember how many times I have forewarned you, my dear Lydia, when at Bath! I told you again and again that you encouraged that Fairly's visits too much." "Captain Fairly!" repeated the wife, putting aside the salts, with more surprise than sorrow, "what, in the name of wonder, has led you to think the Captain has any concern in this good-for-nothing girl's elopement? I only wish you may find she has done no worse! I no more believe she is gone off with him than with the pope. I know more of Captain Fairly than you do; but it is always your way, Jerry, to blame me. Do you think me such a fool as not to have seen it, if he had made love to the girl?" "We will not fall out on that question," replied Mr. Serge; "we have troubles sufficient for the hour. All I have to say is *this*, whether it be Captain Fairly, or any other honourable gentleman of his class, who has robbed me of my child, he shall find his work as unprofitable as those who, as we say, perform their work with 'a hot needle and burnt thread.' Jeremiah Serge has not worked early and late to enrich a *rascal*; nor will I countenance a child who has preferred the protection, of a *rascal* to that of a tender, honest father." He covered his face and wept aloud. Mrs. Serge was silenced, as well as myself. The dejected father was roused from this sorrow by the entrance of the doctor, who told him that Caroline was much easier, and was disposed to sleep. "Blessed be God!" said he, with an expression of gratitude: "One hope remains. But I will go to bed," added he languidly, "for I am strangely disordered, and only a trouble to my friends." Tears again streamed from his eyes; and no one opposed his retreat. We soon followed his example, and sought that repose which was not to be found at Tarefield-Hall: I traced her benign footsteps to Heathcot; and there it was that the spirits of your Rachel Cowley found rest. My dear Mary will expect the sequel of this wonderful business with more than usual curiosity: she shall not be disappointed by her affectionate

Rachel Cowley.

LETTER XLV

From the same to the same.

Tuesday.

On Sunday morning we saw nothing of our disconsolate guests. Mr. Serge was closeted with Sir Murdoch; and Mrs. Serge was too much indisposed to rise before the dining hour. Before I give you the conversation the baronet has just been detailing to his wife and myself, I must tell you, that such is my veneration for Mr. Serge, that I cannot be at peace with my conscience till I have made "l'amende honorable," for the flippancy of my pen in describing him to you on my first seeing him. A few more such lessons as I have had will correct my presumption in judging too soon; and when I am again tempted to laugh at a double chin, or the cut of a man's face, I will remember Sir Murdoch's and Mr. Serge's. The baronet's account of the interview between him and this good creature has so steeled my heart against Miss "Nora," that I wish to leave her on her journey; and for once descend to a vulgarism, and say to you, that if it takes "nine taylors to make a man," I can prove without difficulty, that it would take ninety and nine gentlemen to make such a taylor as Jeremiah Serge. Read, and be incredulous if you can! The conversation began by the baronet's arguments of hope and consolation. "I hope that in time, and with God's help, I shall be comforted," answered Mr. Serge; "but it is not to be expected, that I who am quite an unlettered man, should be so able to meet misfortunes as those who know more. I have endeavoured to do my duty, as well as I was able to perform it; but I fear my ignorance has brought this calamity on my poor child." "How can this be," asked Sir Murdoch, "have you not lived to render your children happy?" "I thought I had," replied he, mournfully, "and perhaps I accuse myself without just grounds; for I dare say, that be a parent ever so wise and learned, if his heart is wrung as mine is, he will think of some failure or other of his own, which may have led to the evil he deplores: however this may be, I cannot help knowing, that my love of peace, and my ignorance have brought me to sorrow. I never liked this Captain Fairly, who is without doubt the betrayer of my poor child; for we found last night a letter which Nora left for her mother, in my wife's night cap. I hated to see this coxcomb perpetually dangling after my wife, and I told her so; but she cried, and asked me whether she had ever given me cause to be jealous. I could not say she had, for I believe there never was a more faithful wife; and moreover, I heard her constantly talking to this puppy about a sweetheart whom he expected at Bath. Some few days before we left that place I met with a friend, who knew something of Fairly's father. He told me, that he had left this young man a pretty estate, and some money; but that he had dissipated his fortune, and was then a gambler and a fortune-hunter. I told Lydia this, but she only laughed, and said my friend had mistaken the matter; for fortune was hunting after Fairly, a rich widow being in love with him. However, by this time, I know *Captain Fairly*," added he, with resentment, "but he does not yet know Jeremiah Serge. I will teach him, ignorant as I am, to know, that the goose is not so easy to pluck as the pigeon. No man is more easily deceived than I am, Sir Murdoch. How should it be otherwise? For to this hour, I have never been able to discover that dishonesty was profitable to a man, even in this world, to say nothing of a better; but when I am tricked by a knave, his business is done with me. I am not twice caught in the same gin. But, Lord help me! I talk as though it was keeping my money that could console me! Alas! what am I the better for riches! One child who has been the prop of my *every* comfort, is sinking into an untimely grave! a second, so trained as to be useless; and the third, who was my pride and pleasure, the property of a villain! I must tell you, Sir Murdoch, all the bitterness of my soul. It has for some time been in my mind, how to make that wealth which Providence has placed in my hands a blessing to my children. I never wished to aggrandize myself with alliances that were above my "cut." Yet I thought my Leonora would not disgrace any man. I sometimes talked with my counsellor and best friend, a *Counsellor Steadman*, on this subject; and I begged of him to look out for me a son in law, who had honour wherewith to meet my honesty, and good sense enough to balance an easy fortune with an uncertain expectation from birth. He sometimes joked at my anxiety; and said my girl would do for a duchess. But knowing I did not wish for a duke, he mentioned a young man, who to me stands higher than the whole peerage. This was your Malcolm, your crown of glory, Sir Murdoch!" The baronet surprised, attempted to speak. "Hear me out," continued he, "before you censure me for looking above me. I knew that you had married my wife's relation, and that with your rank, you had the feelings of a man. Your son had every thing, *but money*; and my child had *with that*, a father whom no man can reproach. So I determined to visit Tarefield, and to take my chance. Hospitality and kindness have received me; and encouraged by them, I ventured to hint my wishes to Mr. Maclairn. But he did not, or as I now know, he could not listen to me. In our ride home from Durham I was explicit with him; and like what he is, he was also explicit with me; and told me, that his hand and his heart had long been plighted to a young lady in this neighbourhood. I will say nothing of this disappointment, nor the shock it gave my mind, on hearing that that very child had abandoned me for whom I would have travelled barefooted through the world to have provided her with such a protector as Malcolm Maclairn. I have now told you *all*, except what will comfort me. Give me your *hand*, Sir Murdoch, for my *heart*. Let me have a share in your blessing: make me useful to your Malcolm's happiness. This is what I ask. It shall not make me proud; but it will comfort me, and be a blessing to my last hour." Miss Lydia entered the room, to say that her sister Caroline wished to see her father; and wringing Sir Murdoch's hand he hastily followed Lydia to the sick room.

I will now leave you to your comments, having to write to our 'crown of glory.' *Adieu, pour le present.*

Rachel Cowley.

LETTER XLVI

From the same to the same.

Ah! flattery!—I see I must go on with my 'pathetic tale.' Therefore I may as well proceed and leave to the flatterers to keep up the connexion. Doctor Douglass was present at the first interview between Mr. Serge and Caroline, and even regulated it. A tender embrace, and an assurance of her being free from pain was all that was permitted; and the poor father satisfied with this, retreated at the doctor's command. Malcolm persuaded him to ride, and they returned not till the placid features of Mr. Serge could bear our kindness. To-day I have seen Caroline; having heard from Mrs. Allen that she was easy and composed.

I was prepared to find her in bed, but not to see her father stretched by her side on the outside of it, thinking he was with his wife. Oh! how fervently do I wish that every girl whom folly and heedlessness may tempt into the same road to ruin which Miss Leonora has taken, could have witnessed, as I did, the pangs which rend a parent's bosom for the desertion of a child! Would to heaven I possessed the invisible belt of fiction, I would reserve it for the sole purpose of making such offenders the unseen spectators of the misery they cause! To judge from the anguish I felt, they would be justly punished! Caroline was supported by pillows in a sitting posture, her countenance still wearing the impression of distress, and the languor occasioned by pain and opiates. Her father was weeping in silence, his face covered. "You will forgive her," said the tender pleader, entirely unmindful of my entrance. "You will, my dear father! Yes, I see you will receive again, this dear, this poor deluded girl!" "I will, I will," said he, sobbing, "I will do any thing, rather than see you grieve, my blessed child! my only hope." "Consider her youth, her inexperience, her beauty," continued the daughter. "Ah! poor creature!" replied the afflicted parent, "I do consider them, and my own incapacity also! These have been her destruction! She is lost, irreparably lost!" "I hope not," answered Caroline: "we are all liable to error, my dear father: no age can secure us always in the right path, without other aids than our own feeble powers; but we may return to duty, we may recover the ground we have lost, and if her husband love her, and what must be that man who could, in his circumstances, fail in affection, all may yet end well." "It can never end well;" answered he, relapsing into agony, "I say she is *undone*, ruined for life! She has united herself to a thief, a base purloiner of another's treasure; and for what? why for the pelf, which is dross to the loser in comparison with a lost child! This rascal is too base, even for hope. This was no boy's trick with him: neither her beauty nor her innocence allured him. She was the casket in which I kept my money; and had she been the foulest thing in nature, he would have been contented with his prize, so his purpose of wickedness had been accomplished. He is a villain! my Caroline; and whether it had been my wife, or my child, that had opened to him my coffers, it would have made no difference to him. But God help me, what am I doing!" added he, checking his vehemence and sorrow. "Grieve no more, my dear Caroline, all shall be as you direct; only be comforted: this poor girl shall be pitied, shall be received again into a father's arms. She shall not find me unrelenting. She shall be happy if I can make her so, and that will cheer you."

I could not remain in the room any longer: I was totally subdued by the language of nature and affection, and again my heart bitterly reproached the child who could abandon such a father: who had not, in his sharpest pangs of sorrow, uttered one menace, and who, hanging over the sick couch of a dutiful daughter, thought more of her consolation than of his own injuries. I recalled my wish, however; for had Miss Leonora been present, she must have died of compunction; and Caroline has made me charitable. I hope she will live to repent; and repay in some measure her father's goodness.

Mrs. Serge did not appear till the tea hour yesterday. She looked pale, and was for a time silent and sorrowful; but at length she began on the subject of her inquietude. The fugitive was by turns "an ungrateful girl," and "her poor betrayed child;" but what appeared to have made a deep impression on the mother, was the difficulties to which Miss Nora would be exposed in the journey for want of clothes and linen. "She would be such a figure!" and then "for a girl like Nora to be married in such a low life way! She, that might have married in the face of the whole world, even a nobleman, with her fortune!" "That opinion of yours, my dear Lydia," observed Mr. Serge, somewhat dryly, "has, I fear, been too often repeated before Mr. Fairly; and it has had its effect, for it has conquered his dislike *to a brown girl.*" — His lady coloured crimson deep at this remark. — "There is no accounting for his behaviour," answered she; "but if it was money he wanted, I know that he might have had a widow with thirty thousand pounds in her pocket by *holding* up his hand. I must think Nora courted him: his handsome person might, without any discredit to her's, or any woman's choice, have pleased her: however, she might have done worse, Jerry; for after all, Captain Fairly is a gentleman, and belongs to people who can push him forwards in the world: I know he has great relations in the East Indies." "Are you not mistaken, Lydia, as to the place in which this noble captain has friends and connections?" asked Mr. Serge. "Oh no," replied she eagerly, "I have heard him speak many times of a cousin he has at Bombay, who married a nabob, because he would not marry her himself: so in despair she went to the East Indies, and got a husband in a fortnight after she arrived." "I must still think you are out in your geography," replied he, "for I must believe he will never find any friends to acknowledge him, unless at Botany Bay; and upon condition he transport himself thither, my purse shall be open to him." "Lord, Jerry, how cruelly you talk!" answered the weeping wife; "but I know you so well, that I ought not to mind what you say: when you see your poor girl on her bended knees before you, you will forgive and forget." "I have forgiven her, without seeing her on her bended knees," replied he with emotion. "Let her reserve that humility for her heavenly Father: she has offended him in forgetting her duty to me; and this grieves me, Lydia, more than you think." A big tear rolled down his honest face: then turning to Sir Murdoch and his lady, he expressed his concern at having given them so much trouble and vexation; and mentioning his intention of leaving the Hall on Tuesday morning, provided Doctor Douglas did not oppose the measure. I omit the reply made to this declaration. "I have not the smallest doubt," said he, struggling to suppress his tears. "You are good and kind-hearted people, and as such, speak as you mean; but my child wishes to be at Putney, in order to receive and comfort her sister." The doctor observed, that Miss Serge's anxiety to return home would be more hurtful to her than the journey. It was, therefore, settled, that our guests should depart at the time they proposed, which is, however, postponed till Thursday.

My reverence for Mr. Serge has, my dear Lucy, risen within these few last days to veneration. I have even neglected my bounden duty to my dear Sir Murdoch, in order to watch Mr. Serge in his solitary walks in the avenue. We understand each other. He talks to me of his idol Caroline: asks me a thousand questions about Mr. Hardcastle; and wonders that he never heard Counsellor Steadman mention so extraordinary a man! Then he stops, looks in my face, and says with a sigh, "What would I give to see my Caroline as healthy as you, Miss Cowley? But she is as good as you are. If you knew the heart of my child you would love her, and pity me." The tone with which he calls Caroline "his child" is so peculiarly tender, and expressive of his affection for her, that a stranger to him and his family would conclude that his hopes hung on the life of an *only child*: but in his conduct to them all he appears to be governed by one leading principle of affection and indulgence; and the preference he gives to Caroline is the result of that confidence and esteem which his own unsophisticated understanding has discovered to be due to her worth and talents. He calls her sometimes his *Prop*, at another his *Pride*, and his *Boast*; and this morning with a flood of tears, he told me that I could never know what were the advantages he had reaped from having had a child like his Caroline; and he concluded that my father had been *well educated*, by the wisdom he had shown in regard to me; "whereas," added he, "my child has been eyes to the blind, as I may say, in her parents' house."

Farewell! I am going to take an airing with Mr. Serge. Your's, ever,

Rachel Cowley.

LETTER XLVII

From the same to the same.

You are sorry, you say, that the Serges have left Tarefield so soon; and that also my sweet Mary regrets the loss of the best part of my romance, the recovery of Miss Serge's health, and the happiness of the whole family, by the forgiveness of the imprudent Leonora. But I cannot gratify Mary. Heaven in its own time will render to Caroline Serge the meed of suffering virtue. Miss Leonora must first forgive herself, before her father's pardon can be a blessing to her; and if she is ever entitled to his forgiveness, it must be attained by the road of self-reproach and repentance. I can only wish her well through the rugged path, and pray that she may not stumble nor faint in it.

You may think me relapsing into hardness of heart. I cannot help it. My affection for the worthy will have its ascendancy. But I send you the substance of a conversation between me and Miss Serge, which will at once account for my uncharitable sentiments in mentioning the fugitive bride.

Willing to be of some use in the general bustle preparatory to our friends' departure, and to which was added the more than common indisposition of Miss Flint, who has not yet recovered from the consequences of Miss Nora's unceremonious departure, I offered my services to Caroline, who, as being the least exacting, I thought in danger of being the most forgotten. She was quietly and meekly sitting in her easy chair, and alone. She received me with satisfaction. I began to net. The conversation soon turned on her sister, her hopes of meeting her, and effecting an entire reconciliation, and forgiveness of her marriage. "I have only one fear to harass my spirits," added she, "and my efforts to check my impatience augments this fear. I know that my life depends on my being placid; and I may render myself useless to Leonora from my anxiety to serve her." I praised her goodness. "It is my duty only that I can perform," answered she; "and even in my attempts and hopes, as these relate to my sister, I am governed by a still superior principle of action. I well know what my dear father's sorrow will be, when I am removed. He will need comfort, and Leonora has only to use her understanding, and to employ her cares assiduously to be the consoler he will want in the first access of his sorrow: his God and his own piety will then be his consolation, I trust." "And I most fervently hope," replied I, "that your youth and your patience will effect your restoration to health. You will live, I trust, to be a comfort and a blessing to your good father, and all your family. You may reasonably hope to enjoy many years of comfortable existence in this world, before you are recalled to the heaven for which you are so richly prepared." My warm and earnest manner surprised her, I believe; for her eyes swam in tears, and she blushed. "I am indebted to a good and pious aunt, who brought me up," replied she, "for the patience and the peace of mind I have enjoyed under a course of trial, which my youth little expected three years since. How often have I blessed this relation for her lessons, and for an example that has supported me, and which will I hope, still support me to the end."—She checked herself, and then proceeded.

"This aunt," continued she, "might with propriety be called my father's best friend. Left an orphan, and without the means of life, she received him when a mere boy; and supported him as her child. On the death of her husband, who left her rich, she placed my father at the head of the business, and although not more than forty, rejected for his sake several overtures of marriage. She superintended his family; and in the prosperity and tranquillity of my father's life, he was in danger of forgetting, that, 'man was not born to be alone.' He was advancing to the season of old batchelorship, when he married my mother; who is full twenty years younger than himself: she was very pretty, and good-natured: my aunt, as she has told me, feared, on hearing of the marriage, that my father's good genius had forsaken him; but although a mere household drudge, she had understanding to discover that a man of my father's age, with an affluent fortune, and a thriving industry, was not likely when in love to be *controuled by advice.*' The good humour and docility of the young wife soon gained her good will, and her frank confession, that she knew nothing of family management, and was unequal to the direction of one so numerous as my father's, induced Mrs. Massey, my aunt, to give up her plan of living in the country. She retained her post of usefulness; and my mother, delighted by the amusements within her reach, and contented with the idleness of an indulged child, saw with gratitude, rather than jealousy, her authority delegated into the hands of one who never interfered with her pleasures or wishes."

"I was the first born child, and the first serious vexation, that my aunt experienced from my father's marriage. She had hoped to see my mother a nurse; but she was disappointed. I was sent into the *country;* even so far as *Bow;* and two years nursing there returned me to St. Martin's Lane, half stupified with Godfrey's cordial, and ricketty in every joint. Unfortunately my mother, attributing my bad health and feebleness to natural weakness, rather than to improper management, pursued the same line of conduct with my sister Lydia, who was born a more vigorous child; but willing to make some concessions, she placed her at *East Ham,* a little further distant from London, and on Epping Forest. Country nursing would, it is probable, have kept its ground in my mother's good opinion, from the proof Lydia gave of its utility, had it not been for an accident, which happened to my mother, in returning home from visiting her. She was in company with my father, and they were both robbed by a highwayman, who, not contented with their watches and purses, was brutal, and so terrified my mother, that she was in danger of her life, and the consequence was, her losing a male child by a premature birth. Leonora, at my father's request, was reared by a wet nurse at home; and my mother found the nursery in the attic no interruption to her amusements. About this period, fortune augmented my father's abundance: he gained the twenty thousand pound prize in the state lottery; but this accession of wealth made little alteration in our modes of life. My mother preferred a *job* coach to any other, and observed that she had a country house in every good inn within an airing from town. Her early habits of life, and her remoteness from the fashionable world and its follies, had happily secured to her a relish for enjoyments, which, though more common, were less ruinous. She was contented in her own sphere of action, and uncontrouled by my father, who viewing every proof of her kindness and liberality to others through the medium of his own active benevolence, was indulgent to the defects of my mother's mode of being useful. But a death, or a birth, in any family within her knowledge or reach, was the signal for her to desert her own. A stranger might at times have mistaken, in the night, our house for the abode of an accoucheur. Alert and vigilant, my mother obeyed the first summons; and with exultation would detail to my aunt the steps she had trodden, or the road she had passed, in the cares of providing for a funeral, or getting a wet nurse for an infant. I really believe she has answered at the font for more children than she can recollect by their baptismal or sirnames, and has gone more miles to trace the qualifications of a cook-maid for her friends, than a judge goes on his circuit. In a word, all was *pleasure* to my dear mother, that was bustle, hurry, and an exertion of her constant flow of animal spirits. I fear I have spoken too unguardedly of my mother's little foibles," continued Caroline with a modest blush, "for believe me, she has many excellent traits in her character; and even in her mistakes, the goodness of her heart prevails. But I have been led into this confidence in you, Miss Cowley, from the peculiar state of my thoughts as these relate to my sister's unfortunate marriage. I once or twice saw the man to whom she has so unguardedly committed her own happiness, and the tranquillity of her father. I was not pleased with him; for I perceived that he was a designing man, and had already secured by his attentions my mother's good opinion. I now dread his influence as her *son*. The genuine virtue and simplicity of my father's mind, with his indulgence and liberality of temper, will be feeble barriers to oppose to this Captain Fairly's seductions, should it be his pleasure to lead my mother into the snares of dissipation and fashionable life. I have observed, even from the hour the Miss Gudgeons first accompanied Leonora to Putney, the facility with which my mother adopted new ideas of her importance, and new notions in regard to our modes of living. At the last visit which these girls paid us, she offended one of my father's most ancient and respectable friends, by omitting to invite his wife and daughter, because he was a sadler. Her short residence and acquaintance with Lady Gudgeon, at Bath, though fortunately terminated, was not without its bad effects, and I have been concerned to see, from time to time, since our return to Putney, my dear mother assuming with her neighbours more of Lady Gudgeon's manners than they liked; but her cheerfulness and frankness of temper soon conciliated them, and banished from her mind her 'genteel society.' My father will be made wretched," continued the amiable creature, "should this Fairly gain an ascendancy in the family; for I am convinced he is a worthless man, and void of every principle."—She was agitated, and I saw that she with pain suppressed something. "My mother has been much gratified," pursued she, "by my employing my good offices in Leonora's behalf: that is some comfort to me, and it is wrong to anticipate evil. Leonora is now his wife, and I will only think of her future security, not of her present condition." She again paused.——"I was reading this morning," continued she, "the story of the Homespun family, from 'the Mirror:' you will not be surprised, my dear Miss Cowley, after my little detail, that I could not help being struck with the analogy I found between this family and our own. All our mistakes have, as it appears to me, originated from the want of education; I mean of that education requisite to the safety of the individual: one suitable to their rank and place in life. Had my dear father not been raised to such an unexpected accession of wealth, all had been well. My mother's activity would have been confined to the duties of his station, and the care of her children. Our present dangers would not have found a place in the abode of competence and contentment: nor would my father's unambitious mind and simplicity of character, have been an object of censure or of ridicule." I will spare my pen the task of recording my reply to this appeal. You know my wisdom, and if, like Solomon's "it be vanity and vexation of spirit," it served one good purpose, for it led us into a less serious conversation on the subject of female education and female attainments. So leaving to your sagacity to fish out as you can my profound observations, I will send you Caroline Serge's opinions upon these important topics.

"I am no advocate for ignorance," said she, in reply to an observation I had made; "but I am persuaded that the same mode of education cannot be adapted with safety or utility to every girl; and granting all the advantages which you have enumerated as resulting from a cultivated understanding and refined taste, I must still be of opinion, that we should be instructed with a view to the sphere in which we are destined to move, and to the duties to which we are more peculiarly appointed. It is not my father's wealth or connections that could render Leonora happy under the parental roof. Too much refinement for our plain manners has made her discontented and ungrateful; and she will, I fear, be unhappy for life, and a constant source of misery to her parents. Lydia on the other hand,"—She cast down her eyes, and with some hesitation, added,—"may be *their disgrace*; for she has been *too much* neglected. I have many times blessed God, Miss Cowley, for the instructions of my youth: they were such as suited my situation; and they have made me useful to my family, besides having enforced that patience and resignation to the will of God, which my trials have needed, and which the most brilliant attainments might have failed in producing. I have, you see, not considered in this view, the education of a young person, who, like yourself, has been judiciously and well instructed; but that tuition which so often appears to me to neglect, not only what is useful, but what principally constitutes the only object worth attending to; for unless moral discipline goes along with the enlargement of the understanding, and the cultivation of taste, these are nothing; and indeed are often, *more pernicious than ignorance*. It is true," added she, smiling, "that my aunt Massey's lessons were not calculated to render me either polite or accomplished; but there is nothing in household wisdom to pervert the mind, or mislead the imagination. I should have liked to read more than I did; but she was of opinion that I read enough for a girl; and with some vanity, boasted of my arithmetic, when Leonora's talents were mentioned. My bad health, and the confinement to which it has subjected me, have made me fond of reading, and it is with satisfaction that I have seen my father also find amusement from books. He would, I am persuaded, to please me," added she, smiling, "have undertaken to learn Hebrew; but I was contented with his choice of books, and we have confined ourselves to those we understand. Be not surprised, my dear Miss Cowley, that I thus plead in favour of unadorned goodness, and plain sense," continued she. "My father has shown me, that virtue needs not the polish of the world, nor the acquirements of the schools, to make its way to the esteem and reverence of those within the reach of its attractive powers. You have witnessed my father's goodness to his children; and believe me, when I tell you, that his whole life and conversation has been exactly similar to the 'Israelites, in whom there was no guile.' God will comfort and support him when I am removed! But I know, too well for my tranquillity, what he will suffer when I *am* removed, and that thought prevents my being what I ought to be." She checked herself, and wiping away a falling tear, proceeded: "I have not finished my little history," said she smiling, "but I shall tire you; yet it is necessary in order for me to bring forward my conclusions, and to leave with you my confirmed opinion on the subject we have been engaged in." You will supply my answer, Lucy.

"My aunt, in the mean time," continued Caroline, "trained me up to be, as she said, her 'right hand,' and she frequently adverted to her age and infirmities as another and powerful motive, which led her to keep me so much in the domestic way. I was reminded continually of my father's comforts: of the disorder and confusion of such a family as ours, if left without a manager; and hints were from time to time dropped, that my mother had no turn for family affairs, though a good parent, and a good woman. Lydia's indulgences grieved her; but she had too much on her hands, for hourly contests; and my mother was satisfied, that in her day-school she learned enough for her years, and that the kitchen was no worse for her play hours, than any other place. Nora was the idol we all worshipped: she was lively and attractive beyond even the attractive age of infancy: she was the pride of our hearts, and the delight of my father's eyes! Even Mrs. Massey was unable to resist her fascinating vivacity and sweetness of temper; and young as I was, I have remarked the pleasure which beamed from her own comely face, on being told, that the little Leonora was "her very image." I had just attained my fifteenth year, when we lost this good aunt. A will made in my father's favour whilst he was yet a bachelor, put him in possession of her whole property, which I have been told amounted to near thirty thousand pounds.

I have, however, reason for believing that Mrs. Massey had frequently thought of altering the form of her donation; and securing to us her fortune after my father's death: for I remember well hearing her many times say, that my mother was not fit for business, and might be left a young widow. From these remarks she would hastily turn, and descant on the advantages of habits of economy and order; recounting to me the management by which she had seconded her husband's industry, and with what comfort they lived to see their little beginnings of one thousand pounds accumulate, and their business daily flourishing. "However, child," she would add, "your father is in a much more extensive line of business than his uncle ever was; and as his family is a very different one from mine, it behoves him to live at more expence; but that is no reason for being extravagant or careless; and you must never relax in your duty." It may be necessary to tell you that my father's household was larger than is common with people in his class. He carried on an extensive commerce in the wholesale line of his trade, and manufactured his own cloth, in a house of business at or near Wakefield in Yorkshire. In consequence of these engagements, we had in the family several young men as assistants and clerks, who dined at our table, and it was a liberal one. My father had purchased the house at Putney before the melancholy event of my aunt's death, meaning to make it the residence of my mother and his daughters: and in his first depression of spirits for a loss which no accession of fortune could lessen, he declared his intention of quitting business, and living there himself. For a time, however, he found in me, *another Mrs. Massey*, to use his own partial words of praise; for assisted by an old domestic of my aunt's training, I superintended the house in St. Martin's lane, and my dear father still found it his abode of comfort. Leonora was at this period at her school, Lydia, but I need not recapitulate to you her defects! I mentioned to my father my fears for her; and without any opposition on my mother's part, she was permitted to bear me company in St. Martin's-lane. But I was too young for a duenna, and too feeble in health, for endless contests; and warned by the good old woman who directed in the kitchen, that Lydia was too often wanting to have pens mended in the counting house, I gave up a charge for which I was so little qualified. It is nearly three years since my complaint became formidable. Mr. Tomkins, my father's associate in business, married; and I was no longer necessary in St. Martin's-lane. Country air was prescribed, and my father, in order to watch over my health, gave up his commercial concerns and his enjoyment. In every interval of ease, I have endeavoured to win Lydia to some useful application of her hours; but neither my appeals to her reason, nor even her vanity, have been attended with success. Nora's contempt of her has not been unobserved, however; and she has returned this, by fostering in her heart a resentment, which no time will soften; whilst she manifests to me a good will and affection unbounded, but as they are checked by her habits of idleness, and predilection for company, in which she finds herself without restraint. Thus, my dear Miss Cowley, have I vainly endeavoured to be useful to my sisters. Alas! I have found that my arguments are no more understood by beauty, accomplishments, and a *finished* education, than by vulgar ignorance, and rudeness. Too much refinement on the one hand, and too little on the other, having defeated my purpose of seeing them what I desire; the children, and the happy children, of a parent beyond all praise, for purity of heart, and the humble and genuine graces of Christianity. And let me ask you," added she, with animation, "whether in a world like this, and for the accommodation of creatures like ourselves, it is not wisdom, to prefer the lowly but snug cottage, to the sumptuous palace, under every consideration which our reason may suggest in the choice. If the gorgeous structure wants a solid *foundation*, and the cottage a *fence*, I should still seek my safety under the low mud walls, believing that the higher the edifice is, the greater is the hazard."

Mrs. Serge's entrance prevented my reply; and finding she had some directions to give to the servant who followed her, relative to Caroline's clothes, I withdrew. What a loss will this amiable girl be to her family! It is to be lamented, that heaven recalls her from a world, in which she would be an example that good sense is worth something, and more to be coveted than "gold, even than pure gold."

I did not take leave of her without tears. She has promised to write to me if her health permit her.

I forgot to inform you of our parting scene below stairs, and shall preface it, by telling you, that Malcolm now ranks with me amongst my *worthies*. Never talk to me of your Scipio's, your Titus's, and such "heathenish folks," as Deborah used to call them in her indignation, on hearing that they worshipped images, whilst I can produce a mere village swain true to love; and who expects the object of his flame every hour to return, and recompense him for a month of sighs and absence, yet calmly and heroically prepares to devote those hours of joy to the comfort and assistance of the dejected Mr. Serge on the road. The poor man, with a heavy heart, mentioned, that they should find the way much longer to Putney on returning, than when in search of their kind friends. "You have shewn us," added he, "that we have relations, and we shall go home with heavy hearts, counting the miles which separate us; but I shall never forget Tarefield, nor like Putney again." "We part as relations and friends," answered the worthy baronet, taking his hand, "as such we have participated in your recent vexation, my good Mr. Serge; and we are only to be contented by your promising us another, and a longer visit next summer. Tell Leonora I shall not forgive her, 'till I see her in her late nest; and her husband shall pay us for her late desertion, by remaining with us, till we are weary of him and her."

"Thank ye! thank ye!" was uttered by a voice which could not proceed, and which touched me to the very soul. "They wait for us," observed Mrs. Serge, "we must part." Malcolm took Caroline's hand, and asked her whether she had courage to try the phaeton for a mile or two "when you are weary," added he, smiling, "I will be contented with your father." The poor man's features swelled with his emotions. "The Lord be merciful to me!" cried he, "but I verily believe you mean to take care of *us* on the road." "Undoubtedly," answered Malcolm, "and in return I shall expect you will take care of me at Putney for a week." "God will bless you, young man," answered Mr. Serge, in an under-toned voice, and with great solemnity. "This is not the first journey of humanity that will be placed to your account, nor will it be forgotten, that no duty, beyond that of *good will*, has led you to the performance of this second act of charity." Malcolm coloured, and hastened his steps. I am convinced that Mr. Serge alluded to his following his father to town, when for me, he left his home in a condition of weakness, which the son's tenderness saw and compassionated: I have no doubt of

Counsellor Steadman's having mentioned to Mr. Serge, the filial conduct of a young man who so completely won his good opinion, whilst he was with us.

The baronet, thinking it a good opportunity of paying off something from the score of "favours received," persuaded me to take an airing with him after our guests were departed. We drove to Bishop's-Auckland; for since Miss Leonora has made us acquainted with Mr. Type's library, Sir Murdoch reads novels with the avidity and interest of a miss in her teens. Something in Miss Type's manner excited my curiosity. On inquiring whether all the volumes had been returned which had been placed to Miss Serge's account, she replied with a smile in the affirmative, adding, that she hoped the young lady would in her turn find the things she had sent with the books as exact. An explanation followed, and I found that Miss Nora had judged it expedient to use my name instead of her own, in her contrivance to secure for her journey a change of linen, and the girl with some confusion of face told me that, she thought the gentleman at the Mitre had been my lover from what he had said.

So now leaving my dear Mary to consider at her leisure of the marvellous and manifold talents necessary to effect the emancipation of a young lady of sixteen or seventeen, from the galling yoke of parental prudence, and the insipid security of a parental roof, I shall conclude this letter; sincerely congratulating her on the little acquaintance she has with cunning, ingratitude, and a courage which sets at defiance, even a life of misery, for the gratification of having for an hour, "her *own mind.*" Not doubting, but Mrs. Fairly will soon conclude the lesson, by publishing the succeeding volume, under the title of "The too late Repentance." Heaven preserve you, my dear girls, and believe me sincerely your's,

Rachel Cowley.

LETTER XLVIII

From Miss Cowley to Miss Hardcastle.

I never shall, my dear Lucy, attempt to conceal from you the state of my spirits. You judged right. I was dejected by the contents of Horace's last letter. His account of Lord William's recent danger, by the sudden bursting of an abscess on the lungs, and the depression of mind with which Horace wrote the account of this dreadful alarm, could not be balanced by the more flattering hopes with which he finishes his letter. He says, that the patient is relieved, and that the physicians are of opinion, that his life may be prolonged by this effort of nature.

But thoughts will intrude Lucy. Horace continually over the couch of a person in Lord William's situation, is not an image which cheers my serious hours. I believe that few medical men now refuse their concurrence in the opinion that consumptions are contagious, particularly to those who are young. It has been, and must be, a matter of surprise and regret to me, that Mr. Hardcastle has not participated with me in these apprehensions; but on *no* consideration would I wish him to be alarmed at this moment; being certain, that *none* would induce Horace to leave his friend at this juncture. I will therefore imitate him in his virtue, and I beg you will do the same, and leave the event to that Providence which has hitherto preserved his health, and witnessed his perseverance and fortitude in the exercise of his duty. I frankly confess that I have not been altogether your *Beatrix*, since the receipt of Horace's last letters; and the absence of the Serges, with that of my friends from the Abbey, has left me more leisure, than has been useful to me; but knowing my remedy, I have applied to it; and I am at present Sir Murdoch's pupil for painting in oils: he encourages me: and I am employed; the Heartleys are, however, returned, and my spirits are returned with them. Tell Mary she is to give full credit to Alice's news of her uncle's triumphs at Hartley-pool. He is become a beau, and a young man, and could we manage to keep him easy in regard to Miss Flint, we should all be contented with him; but he is too anxious for her to keep long his good looks, which, to say the truth, are beyond any I expected to see, for he is absolutely handsome with his *ruddy* face. Malcolm returned last night; and you, as we did, will expect Putney news. He saw poor Leonora only once: she was indisposed when he left his good friends, but Captain Fairly had several times shown himself to the *modest rustic*. Malcolm, was by no means pleased with him. He says that, except a showy person, which may be called a handsome one, he could not discover a single attraction in this man, which was likely to captivate a girl of Leonora's description; for he is cold, formal, and affected in his manner; and announces the little he has to say with a pomposity which diverted him, and which it was astonishing could have escaped Leonora's ridicule. But he thinks the captain is acting a new part with these simple people, and he asserts, that, Fairly has worn the buskin, or at least, has studied for the stage. Malcolm very discreetly took care to be absent the first day the offending daughter was received at Putney; but judging that the interview would leave Mr. Serge dispirited, he returned in the evening before the new married couple had left the house, which they did, it appears, in order to their finally quitting the Adelphi-Hotel, for Putney, where Malcolm left them. "On entering the drawing room," continued our favourite, "I found only Mrs. Serge with the captain, and a sort of awkward introduction followed. The captain appeared impatient for his lady's departure, who with her father was with Miss Serge; and expressed in high-flown terms, his apprehensions lest his dear Leonora should be completely ill, with a day of such fatigue and trial, for her weak and delicate spirits. I thought him an awkward hypocrite." "Oh! do not fear!" answered the mother, with more tartness of manner than I had yet perceived; "Nora will bear this day's fatigue as well as she did her journey to Scotland; though, to say the truth," added she, "I do not think her *complexion* improved, by travelling post for so many miles; and unless rest restores her colour, you will be in danger of renewing your preference of Lydia's fair skin and hair." She laughed, but it was obvious that more was meant by this observation, than I could understand; the captain, however, probably did; for with a smile he reminded her, that all stratagems were lawful in love and war. "That is more than I will allow," answered she, colouring; "and I must needs think, that a battle or a wife, so gained, *show* more *cunning* than *courage*; however, let this pass, you have succeeded; and I trust you will be happy with your 'Nut-brown Maid.' The captain spouted some poetry in reply; and Mrs. Serge with a look of softened resentment remarked, that he well understood the way to a woman's heart, and she had no doubt of his knowing how to keep Nora's. The door opened, and Mr. Serge entered the room with his weeping daughter. Malcolm hastily retreating into the inner apartment, heard her sobs and adieus. The next day, she took possession of her deserted nest; but was too ill to join the family at their repasts. Malcolm saw her, however, for five minutes, when he took his leave of Caroline, who has wonderfully supported herself during this scene of vexation. He was commissioned to say all that was cordial and kind on the part of the harrassed Serges; but they could not write."

We are, my dear Lucy, becoming *lambs* at Tarefield Hall: Miss Flint could not settle for the night, without sending Warner with her compliments to Mr. Maclairn, with inquiries after his health and Mr. Serge's family. Malcolm, whose heart is that of a lamb, also coloured at this unexpected civility; and he very handsomely sent his acknowledgments, and Miss Serge's particular respects to her fellow sufferer. So true is it, that "soft words turn away wrath," that I verily believe Malcolm listened with pity to his mother's account of Lucretia's sinking health and spirit. I, wisely resolving to profit from this temper of charity, have been in the invalid's room for more than an hour this morning. Lady Maclairn is relieved by these measures, and poor Miss Flint often appears amused by our chat. But it is incredible with what patience she bears the pain in her knee, which is excruciating at times, and prevents her sleeping for nights together. Who could have believed that pain and sickness would have rendered Miss Flint patient and submissive! As it is a bitter remedy, Lucy, so it ought to be an efficacious one; and it is our own fault when it proves useless. Believe me cheerful and well, for indeed I am both; and I am going to the Abbey this evening to exult with *the happy, and* to be happy.

Your's, affectionately,
Rachel Cowley.

LETTER XLIX

From the same to the same.

Your confession, my dear Lucy, with my own, shall be placed aside; but within our reach, in order to be useful when we are again so absurd as to yield to the despondency of anticipated evils. Your brother is well; Lord William gaining ground; and we will be cheerful and contented. Mr. Hardcastle's letter agrees with mine; and whether the physician's hopes be or be not well grounded, we will be thankful, that the interesting patient is relieved from a portion of his suffering, and Horace from the immediate pangs of seeing him expire.

I am just returned from inspecting the contents of two large boxes sent from town, by order of Jeremiah Serge, Esq. "To Sir Murdoch Maclairn, at Tarefield-Hall." A short note from his lady specified, that having recollected that the tea equipage which she had seen at Tarefield was the property of Miss Flint, she had presumed to hope, that the one which gratitude had signed with the initials J. L. S. would find favour at the Hall, and be received by Sir Murdoch and Lady Maclairn, as a mark of their love, and as a tribute of their sense of the kindnesses they had met with under their hospitable roof. Caroline's style was obvious in this note.

All that fashion and wealth have suggested as an appendage to the tea table, successively appeared in plain but highly-finished plate. The other box contained a superb set of Derbyshire china; each piece so accurately painted with views taken from the romantic scenery with which that part of England abounds, that I conceive it to be an outrage on taste to use them, as they would embellish the first cabinet in Europe. Sir Murdoch, as I fancied, looked more oppressed than delighted by this munificent proof of Mr. Serge's gratitude; for surveying the costly urn, &c. &c. he gravely observed, that *wealth* had made Mr. Serge *profuse*, if such were the common returns he made for common civilities. A small parcel directed to Malcolm diverted his attention from pursuing this train of thought; for with an elegant gold watch, and a chain loaded with trinkets, were letters from the family; and the one addressed to the baronet, which was somewhat in the *onion* form, being produced, he retired with his share of the present.

In my next you shall see our joint labours; for we have conquered our reluctance to receiving the offerings of pure good will and kindness; or rather these are forgotten in our admiration of a being whose good will is more gratifying. Mrs. Allen has already begun her share of copying the letters from Putney. So peace be with you! I am going *to be good*, and supply her absence in Miss Flint's room.

Rachel Cowley.

In continuation.—We have agreed, that, as Mrs. Serge wrote so much in a *hurry;* and that as we are ourselves so much in a hurry to gratify your curiosity, it may suffice to give the substance of Mrs. Serges's letter to her "dear cozin." She refers her for particulars to "Jerry;" and is contented with rejoicing, that matters are amicably settled: not in the least doubting but that Captain Fairly will soon gain her husband's good opinion, he being a "wery sensible man." She is so engaged in shopping for Nora, that she has hardly an hour she can call her own; and what with a change of servants, and one thing and another, she finds herself quite fatigued; but Mrs. Fairly was not well enough to order her new dresses; and it was necessary they should be in hand, against her seeing the captain's friends. This, I think, is all that is worthy of notice in Mrs. Serge's epistle, except her kind compliment to me, in which she assures me that she shall insist on having the pleasure of seeing me her guest, as soon as Mrs. Fairly is settled in London; and that with the young bride and Miss Cowley, she promises herself much pleasure in the winter months; for Nora might be said to be a stranger in town, as well as Miss Cowley.

Caroline's short note to Malcolm is written in a style of affection. She calls him her *"Dear brother,"* and requests him to present to Miss Heartley the watch, &c. she had sent. "Her acceptance of this trifle," adds she, "will convince me, that she admits my claims to your friendship, and that she will pardon me for using a title, which Malcolm Maclairn sanctions; and which she frankly confessed, it gave her pleasure to use, although attended with regrets too selfish for Miss Heartley's indulgence." She concludes with wishing that she had seen Alice; but adds, "your affection for her at once bespeaks her worth; and she will deserve the happiness which awaits her."

The following letter you have entire. Not a syllable of Mr. Serge's shall be lost.

LETTER L

Putney, October the 11th, 1790.

"My good Sir Murdoch and Cousin,"

"I send you with my kind love, a small tribute of my gratitude, the sentiments of which I shall carry with me to my grave, for all your hospitable cares of us, when with you; and above all, for your pity and compassion towards my dear sick child. I have only to say on this subject, that not you, nor any under your roof, will ever live to repent of your kindness to Caroline; for there never was a young creature who better deserved the consideration of good people.

"You must take the will for the deed, if we have blundered in regard to the things we have sent to your worthy lady; but Caroline thought her mother had judged very properly; and was certain you would be pleased with any marks of our affection, seeing we are not those, who do one thing and mean another; and if the fashion of these things should not happen to suit your fancy, the fault is not my wife's, for she took a great deal of pains to get what was tasty, that I must say; and Lydia would go to the world's end to serve a friend.

"I have had a meeting with my poor Nora, and my fine spark of a son in law: it was just as my dear Caroline said it would be. I never felt so uncomfortable in my life as when I saw my poor girl attempting to speak to me, and unable to utter a word! I was like a dying man: I could hardly breathe. What then must she have suffered, Sir Murdoch? Seeing, she had left *me* for another's protection, not I *her*: but women have a great advantage over us, for tears relieve them; and although I have shed many, and found them serviceable, yet on this occasion I could only compare my eyes to dry springs. Well, I sent her to Caroline's room, where I knew she would find comfort. So then my gentleman began to talk of his *love* and his *honour*; but I stopped him short, and in so many words told him, that I would not give him a cast off brass button for his whole stock of either of these articles. 'A little honesty, *Mr.* or Captain Fairly,' added I, 'would have pleased me better. I am a plain, and it may be, in your eyes, an ignorant man. I see no honour in running away with another man's child, any more than with his purse; nor any love in cheating a silly young girl of her principles of duty to her parents, and reducing her to a life of sorrow and repentance. However, it is no longer time to think of this: what is done, is done: she must stand the hazard. The business now is, to make the *best of what is done*. You knowing my calling and station in the world, and need not fear on that score: Pray tell me, what is *your* calling, Sir: What are your prospects and pursuits? I am told, you have sold your commission, and spent your father's estate.' He looked confounded, said it was unfortunately true, the indiscretions of youth had dissipated his means, and bad health had obliged him to quit his regiment. But he trusted, that at thirty years of age, he had gained experience, and that he might yet live to obliterate from the world's recollection, the follies of a youth of sixteen, committed to his own direction, with a sword by his side, and a feather in his hat. 'Well,' said I, 'this is what *I call* honest. Now tell me, what is become of your estate: your father left it to you, and I should like to see it reclaimed, and in your hands, to leave it to a son, who might be made prudent by your experience: I am not a hard-hearted man, Mr. Fairly, nor are you the first I have assisted, whose fortune was out at the elbows. This estate I will redeem, provided you are content to reside on it, and on condition, that I know your debts to their full extent.' He assured me that these were trifling; but confessed that the estate was mortgaged for nearly its full value. 'No matter,' returned I, 'I will not recede from my purpose: I did not like your trade at Bath: try whether farming will not employ you more profitably: be kind to your wife, and I will pass over all offences.'—He thanked me, and again talked of his honour, saying he was ready to give me any securities I wished, for my daughter's future provision. 'I want none from you,' answered I, 'beyond that love and faith you have given her before your Maker; for the rest, *I shall be her security*. My daughter, by her imprudent conduct, has made over *to me* the care of providing for her children; and they shall not be beggars, if I can prevent it. A fine tale indeed would it be, to put on Jeremiah Serge's grave-stone, that he trusted the property of hard-earned industry and the future means of supporting his family, to a girl of sixteen, who threw herself away!' My gentleman was angry; but I again stopped him short: 'You will do well to remember,' said I, 'that I am a man who have made my way in the world by a very simple rule in arithmetic, two and a nought will never make three in my reckoning: a laced jacket will never supply the want of a good lining. Do you take heed to merit my kindness, and leave to me the provision for my daughter. Your good conduct will make me generous. Till I know more of you I will be just, and every three months Nora shall have one hundred pounds to pay your baker's and butcher's bills. But I warn you, not to trust to me for being an easy fool to manage. I repeat it, Mr. Fairly, I am not an ill-natured man, although a very firm one on some occasions. Seeing but a very little way before me, I see, perhaps, pretty clearly, what it is my duty *to do*; and when I see *that*, nothing can turn me from forming it. If you want a little ready cash, say so, I will supply you, as I would any man in need; and will forget, if I can, that my money probably pays for the post horses that carried my child to Gretna Green.' So I put into his hand an hundred pound bank-note, which he took with a lower bow than I could have made for ten times the sum, to a man I had cheated. Our conference finished, by my saying that I thought my house a more suitable residence for his young wife, than either a public one, or private lodgings, till his own was ready; and offering my hand, I told him that it depended on himself to find a father under its roof. I thought he looked ashamed, and his hand trembled so, that brought to my mind more forcibly my blessed Master's commands, 'If thy brother sinneth against thee, seven, and seventy-times-seven, thou shalt forgive him.' And, after all, Sir Murdoch, where is the comfort of an unrelenting temper? This man may turn out a good husband, and repay my forgiveness of him an hundred-fold by his kindness to my poor heedless girl. He may, if he will, make a worthy man, and a good father, and be a comfort to me: at any rate, I have done my duty, and pleased my blessed Caroline. She told me this very morning, that she was certain I had secured the approbation of my own conscience, and the favour of God, by my goodness to Leonora; and that my conduct had given her a joy which this world had not the power to lessen. Oh! if you could but see, and hear her! But she is going where only she can be known and glorified!

"I shall not finish this letter to-day, as I must first see Counsellor Steadman, who will write to you by this conveyance. You will have from him the business now before us, and I shall expect your answer to be speedy."

October the 12th.

"My friend the Counsellor assures me, that he has so explained my views and wishes, that you will not be offended, nor be able to misunderstand my intentions. I shall therefore altogether waive the subject, and finish my paper with my own cares and troubles; for it is the only relief I find to disburden my mind of the multitude of thoughts that oppress me, and I cannot help believing that my gracious and merciful God, knowing that I should want a friend to support me in my trials, has opened to me a road in which my ignorance and weakness would meet with help and kindness.

"Poor Nora has not got up her spirits yet; she looks sadly, and seems more pained than encouraged by my pity for her. Poor fool! She is like a young bird, Sir Murdoch, who, in too much haste to try its wing, has just reached a limed twig in sight of the nest it so heedlessly quitted; and she now, poor girl, like it, sorrows, and thinks of the comfort she had with us. My wife says that the Captain is very fond of her, and if all be gold that glitters, I am to believe that he doats upon her; but once *bit* twice *shy*, is the maxim uppermost with me, when the Captain is concerned. Fine words and scraps of poetry do not convince me that he loves his wife better than I did mine, in the honey moon, as it is called; and I am sure my Lydia never shed a tear then, nor for many and many months after her name was Serge. I told poor Nora this morning, that it grieved me to see her so dejected, and that it was time for her to be cheerful, as I had no other intention in my proceedings, than to show her my unabated affection, and to secure her comforts. Poor creature! she burst into tears, and said I was killing her by my kindness! God will, I trust, forgive me, Sir Murdoch, for my heart smote me at the moment; but I could not help *cursing inwardly* the rascal who had robbed me of such a child! My dear Caroline is yet my consolation. She tells me, that Nora will be better soon; and accounts for her present poor health in a way that cheers me. Fairly says he loves children; that is a good sign; and I think there cannot be found a man who does not love his own; so we will hope that he will settle into a family man and a good husband, and then I may live to forget my injuries, and to bless his children. God Almighty grant it may be so! prays fervently your sincere and dejected friend,

"Jeremiah Serge.

"P. S. All here desire their kind love. We wish to hear from you, and to learn that Miss Flint is mending. God bless you, and your kind-hearted compassionate lady! You are a happy man, Sir Murdoch! You have indeed a helpmate! Would to God all wives could be called so."

In order to avoid prolixity, I have suppressed a few of Miss Cowley's letters, which were written during the course of a month, as those contain nothing essentially necessary to the narrative before me; and are chiefly addressed to Miss Howard, and written in Italian and French, with a view to making these languages familiar to her. But I am so much influenced by Miss Cowley's opinions, that I cannot persuade myself that I could better oblige my readers, than by recommencing my allotted work, with the following letters sent to Miss Hardcastle with her friend's usual punctuality.

LETTER LI

From Miss Serge to Miss Cowley.

Putney, Dec. 6.

"You have, my dear madam, been so minutely informed of every occurrence that has taken place here since our return home, that I have with less reluctance deferred writing to you than the kindness of your request of hearing from me would otherwise have justified. I hasten, however, with satisfaction to avail myself of an hour of comparative ease and tranquillity of mind, to acquit myself, in part, of the debt of gratitude so justly your due, and, with my poor, but sincere thanks for all your goodness, to relieve my thoughts by a further communication of those disquietudes, which still prevent my being *what I ought to be*.

"It will not surprise you to hear, that in my hours of solitude, my thoughts recur to Lady Maclairn's affectionate greetings and tender solicitudes; to Mrs. Allen's soothing cares; to Miss Cowley's encouraging smiles and animating conversations. These thoughts will intrude; and I cannot yet treat them as intruders. Yet I have my father: but *that father* is a source of my deepest sorrow! I see he is deceiving himself; that he cherishes the most fallacious of hopes: he thinks me better, because my pains are less acute. He sees not, that nature, worn out in the unequal struggle, is passively yielding to the inevitable, though still suspended stroke; and I have not the courage to tell him, that his Caroline is every hour hastening to her grave. A fever which eludes his notice, and profuse nightly perspirations, to which he is a stranger, must soon be terminated. I am neither deceived, nor alarmed. I have made an acquaintance with my conqueror, which has stripped him of his terrors, and I find that aspect which is so appalling and so hideous when viewed from afar, and through the medium of this world's pleasures and gratifications, not unfriendly to the weary sufferer.

"I have weighed and measured my portion of painful existence, with that of the sinner, who, like 'the giant,' runneth his race to destruction;' and I am thankful. I have entered again and again into that seat of judgment, which none but the eye of my Maker can pervade: neither remorse nor fear assail me. I have been *an heedless* child; but never *a hardened one*, with my earthly parent; and how has he loved me! and can I for a moment tremble at the thought of meeting face to face, my Heavenly Father, my Almighty Friend, who knoweth that I am but dust before him; and who has yet upheld me with tenderness and love? No, my dear Miss Cowley: imperfect as my services have been, manifold as have been my omissions of duty, I cannot forget that I have for my salvation a God of infinite mercy and goodness; and in hope I shall calmly resign up my spirit into his hands. I have been led into these reflections by the considerations of that gracious providence which has permitted me to see my dear father somewhat relieved from his late vexations, and which hath allowed to me the means of being useful to my sister. All has been done that we can do for her comfort. We must leave the future to her own conduct, and the principles of the man to whom she has so unguardedly trusted her happiness. I wish to entertain a favourable opinion of Mr. Fairly; but I am uncandid, or he is unworthy. He disgusts me by his attentions and flattery to my poor mother, his fulsome and ridiculous fondness to his wife before my father. With me he affects a pragmatical gravity and importance, talks of my wonderful wisdom, patience, and fortitude, 'till he convinces me, that I am peevish and irrascible. Poor Lydia is either overlooked or reproved by him, with an impertinence which my mother and Leonora ought to check. The consequence is, that she detests him; and has moped in her own room till she is unwell. She grieves also, poor thing! for Willet's removal from the family. This young woman, whom you will recollect was with us at the Hall, was a favourite with my mother, and in fact Lydia's companion and friend: indeed, we all liked her as a useful well-behaved young person. Willet, however, took offence on finding at our return hither, a house-keeper installed in office, by Mrs. Tomkins, at my father's and mother's request, during our absence: she was impertinent, and not chusing to make concessions, or to accept of the station my mother chose for her, she quitted her good lady and her dear Miss Lydia for another service. I have been a gainer by this change in our administration. Willet was too lively to be useful to me; and we have gained a prize in the good woman whom Mrs. Tomkins recommended to us. Mrs. Thornton has so pleased my dear father, that he has in his fond consideration promoted her to a place of more trust than the housekeeper's room—she is now my constant attendant; and her daughter superintends below stairs with great regularity and diligence.

"My mother has been absent from home nearly a fortnight. She accompanied Mr. Fairly and Nora to his house, near Chelmsford in Essex; with the intention of seeing that it was a suitable abode for her daughter. I was much gratified with my sister's reply on the occasion. She said she should be happy with any accommodations in the country. I suspect poor Nora has in the course of a few short weeks discovered that she has gained but little by exchanging the yoke of her tender and generous father, for the chains of wedlock, a regimental suit, and a handsome man. She is not in spirits. Since her departure she has written twice to my father: her expressions of gratitude, paid him for his money, and I believe they were dictated by her feelings. She mentions the house as being all she wishes, but that her too *fond* and *anxious* husband thinks it stands in need of repairs, and that it cannot be made a suitable residence for her for less than *fifteen hundred pounds*. The money was instantly advanced; and Leonora, in her second letter informed us, that Mr. Fairly had consented to live at the farm till the house was ready for them. There was an appearance of content and triumph in this letter which delighted me. She spoke of her plans of furnishing it *neatly*: of her garden; and of the happiness she hoped to find in a cottage orné.

"Yesterday, instead of my mother, whom we expected, arrived a letter from her, dated from Reveland Park, the seat of a rich nabob, called Anthony Dangle, Esq. His house borders on Mr. Fairly's little estate, and his lady, recently married, was one of Nora's school companions. My poor dear mother writes in raptures of the grandeur and style of Reveland Park: the table, the society, and the politeness of the young mistress of the mansion, who at eighteen or nineteen, purchased with her beauty and accomplishments, the state of an Asiatic princess, and a husband of forty, already a cripple with the dead palsy. Leonora will be her guest for some time: in the exultation of my mother's heart she hopes they will keep her till her own '*little box*' is ready; for Nora is adored at the Park. Can you blame me, if my anxious and apprehensive mind recurs to the story of the Homespun family? Alas! no: you are too judicious not to see the danger of such connections as these, to *my mother*."

"This letter, my dear Miss Cowley, will not amuse you, but it will make its appeal to your good nature: you will think of the invalid who has beguiled three or four tedious days of their allotted dullness, in writing it: you will think you see her raising her languid eyes to heaven, whilst she breathes out a petition for your happiness; and you will think with kindness of the grateful and obliged

"Caroline Serge."

"P. S. I shall say nothing of my *brother*, Malcolm Maclairn. Ah! would to heaven I had a more legitimate claim to use that title, than even his kindness has given me. What a difference in Nora's fate would such a man have made! It is not possible for me to tell you, how gentle how humane, his conduct was to us on the road. But he is a good and a virtuous man; and may the Almighty bless him! My father writes to Sir Murdoch, or to him, I believe; he desires to have my letter to enclose. I expect to see my mother in a few days, and Mrs. Tomkins will be with us to-morrow evening, to pass some time at Putney."

LETTER LII

To Malcolm Maclairn, from Mr. Serge.

"My dear young Friend,"

"Having received from your good father more compliments than I asked, and less information than I wanted, relative to the plans in which you were engaged with Mr. Wilson, when I was at Tarefield, I have taken my measures in my own way, and with better success; for Wilson and I have managed the business without compliments or demurs; and you are fairly *lurched*, if you be a young man too proud to accept of a kindness from a true friend. Hoping you will see the drift of my meaning, I send you a draft on my banker for a thousand pounds: it is placed in your name, and herewith you have his acknowledgment. Get married and settle at once: have no fears: I will take care of my farm and my farmer. Let your nest be well lined: I send the bill for that intent; meaning to take care myself of all without doors. Your answer to this will either break the thread of our love, or join it till death; for it will either show me, that you do not know Jeremiah Serge, or that he does not know Malcolm Maclairn. However, guessing where the "shoe will pinch," I will say that when I want my money again I will ask you to pay it. And in the mean time receive a good interest for it in your good will and kindness. So may God prosper you, and my money thus employed!

"I am your loving friend,

"Jeremiah Serge."

[*Miss Cowley's pen is employed in what follows.*]

I was with Lady Maclairn when her son read her this letter. I cannot describe to you the various changes of her countenance, whilst he was so doing. Her lips trembled, and with difficulty she asked him whether Sir Murdoch would be satisfied to see his son established in life by Mr. Serge.

Malcolm answered that his father left him to act as his own judgment directed: that he had convinced him of the probability of being able to repay his generous friend, and that it was in fact a good speculation for Mr. Serge. "But," added he, "I am not governed altogether by this consideration in my purpose of accepting Mr. Serge's kindness. I am not too proud to receive favours; nor so mean as to court them. The voluntary offering of an honest and generous heart shall be received with a frank and honest gratitude, and I may live, my dear mother, *to give*, as well as *to receive* benefits. At any rate I am not worthless, and my benefactor will not have to blush for his predilection in my favour; for I shall never forget his kindness. And the prospect! my dear Miss Cowley," added he, seizing my hand as if it had been Alice's, "is it not too alluring for romantic scruples, and a fastidious pride to combat." I smiled; and he now eagerly ran over the advantages which would ultimately accrue from the Wereland Farm: expatiated on the happiness before him; and in the most unqualified manner adverting to Miss Flint's dissolution as a contingency that would not break his heart, he drew a picture of domestic peace and comfort, to which his affection gave the most glowing colours. "We shall then taste the blessings of union and love undisturbed," said he. "My Alice will reverence and serve my mother; and we shall see her smile, and bless our infants." The poor mother answered only with her tears. "Why do you weep?" asked he, with tenderness. "It is because I fear, my dear Malcolm," replied she, "that this cup of joy will never reach my lips." "It is I that ought to have this doubt to check my present contentment," answered he seriously, "whilst I see my mother wasting her health and spirits on — —." She prevented his finishing; and with a gentle smile asked him, whether he had seen Mr. Wilson. He replied in the negative, adding that he was then going. "Do not forget to tell your friends," said she, "that Lady Maclairn means to write to Mr. Serge, and to thank him for having rendering her son happy." Malcolm kissed her glowing cheek, and withdrew. "Poor fellow!" said she, the instant the door closed, "how little does he know that nothing on this side of the grave can make *his mother happy*! I see your surprise, my dear Miss Cowley," added she, weeping, "you are not prepared with the frankness with which I now confess that there has been *for years* a canker worm in this bosom, which has not only destroyed my peace, but which has also tainted my *very face* by its baleful influence. You are yet a stranger to the woman before you; notwithstanding that penetration which has shown you that she is not what she *wishes to appear*. I have perceived your suspicions; and in a thousand instances, have marked your but too accurate conclusions. I have had lately to struggle, not only with my secret sorrows, but with the acute sense of being suspected *as a deceitful woman* by that being to whom I stand indebted for the only comfort of my life: by my husband's friend and consoler! Yet, Miss

Cowley, my soul is yearning to convince you that it is honest and sincere. I must explain to you the causes which have imposed upon me a conduct of duplicity and deceit. I want a friend, Miss Cowley: yes, I want a friend, in whose faithful bosom I may with safety place a secret that oppresses my own, and which must destroy me. I have for some time resolved to take this step. You will, I think, be disposed to grant me your compassion, if the narrative I mean to place before you should exclude me from your friendship and esteem." She spoke with so much energy and feeling, that I was confounded, and remained silent. "I distress your generous mind," continued she, "but recollect your conduct; recall the numberless instances in which your candour and goodness have been exerted to spare the too conscious dissembler. I will only say a few words more: justice to myself demands them! Had not your firm refusal of Philip Flint rendered my purpose needless, you would have known his mother before you had been a week under this roof. I will not say what were my feelings when I found that this trial of my strength was spared me! You once invited me to call you *my daughter*," added she, renewing her tears. "Good God! could you at that moment have seen my heart! Could you but have conceived what then passed through my very soul! You were the child of my husband's fond and grateful love! You had saved him! But I was unworthy of you!" I am not made for moments of this kind, Lucy. I could not speak: but hiding my face in her extended arms, I sobbed forth my feelings.

In continuation.—Lady Maclairn has this moment left me. I was shut up all yesterday in my apartment with a cold in my head, which you will place to the real cause. Sir Murdoch and Mrs. Allen made some remonstrances on my insisting that they should keep their engagements to dine at the Abbey. And you will judge that my time was fully engaged by the manuscripts I now send you.

Lady Maclairn took her tea with me, and with composure and dignity of manner, she said, "I see, my dear Miss Cowley, that I have taxed your sensibility severely. You are now acquainted with the unfortunate Harriet Flamall, and are now qualified to judge of her hopes and pretensions to your kindness." 'You are an angel,' exclaimed I, with honest fervour. 'Patience and suffering have made you one, even before your time.' She mournfully shook her head. "I gratefully welcome the sentiment which has urged the misapplied epithet," said she. "I accept with joy and comfort the friendship which dictated it. *I know Miss Hardcastle.* Do you, my dear Miss Cowley, prepare her for her knowledge of *me*. Tell her, that you have received me as a guest worthy of your pure bosom. Send her the manuscripts, and ask her whether two hearts will not be needful to shelter mine from the oppression under which it groans. The dread of having those papers in my possession," added she, "has frequently tempted me to destroy them. Yet I wish to leave some memorial behind me, to witness that my soul abhorred deceit, and that even under the cruel yoke of it, my principles were firmly those which rectitude teaches. The peace and honour of my husband and son were of too much consequence to be hazarded by my impatience under the dependence to which my own weakness had reduced me. Miss Flint's caprices and temper have been to me *petty evils*; and my conformity to her will has been amply recompensed by the reflection that I have served as a barrier, although a weak one, to passions that would have betrayed her more to censure and reproach. She wanted not my brother's arguments to mislead her, but she was a stranger to his artifices. And to whom but myself was it owing that she knew the betrayer of her integrity and honour? Can you any longer be surprised that I have yielded up to motives so powerful, that independence, which under every privation of fortune I should have called *blessedness* to the life I have passed under this roof. Oh, you know not, Miss Cowley," added she, weeping bitterly, "what I have endured! But what was I, if not useful in contributing to Sir Murdoch Maclairn's comfort and happiness! I had deceived him, and imposition was my *hard* duty. How often have I wished that my *death* could have been as beneficial to him, as a life miserable, though devoted to his service!"

You will love and reverence this woman, Lucy. I am certain you will. Sedley will give you this packet. You will understand my caution. I have written to Mary in French, expressly to prevent her inquiries. Let me know that the manuscript is safe in your hands, and that you concur with your perhaps too impetuous,

Rachel Cowley.

P. S. We were reading a beautiful work of Mrs. Inchbald's, called, "The Simple Story," when the vagrants returned. Red eyes and defluxions in the head are the least of these tributes which this novel merits. Ours escaped all further inquiry.

Manuscript intended, for Sir Murdoch Maclairn, from his Wife, and sent to Miss Hardcastle by Miss Cowley.

The vows of fidelity, of obedience, of love, and gratitude, which the obscure Harriet Flamall plighted at the altar with you, my Maclairn, were registered in heaven; and I am prepared to answer undismayed, the inquiry which will be made relatively to my *performance* of *my duties as your wife*. Yes, I am prepared and God and man will acquit me of having deviated from my duty in the course of *that honourable character*. But to what tribunal shall I appeal, when called upon to answer to the charge of deceit, of imposition, of falsehood! Of having imposed on thy generous confidence, and of having worn a *name* and a title to which I had *no right*, and which I have *contaminated*? Is there not a refuge for the penitent? Has not the Almighty promised to forgive his contrite erring children; and will Maclairn's noble mind, refuse pity and compassion to an offender whom he loves? *He cannot*: for it is his delight to walk in the path his Maker hath appointed, and to honour him, by imitating him who is perfect in his goodness. The history of my life will contain all that I have to urge in extenuation of my errors. I am induced to place it before you, by the hope, that it may produce on your mind a conviction, that I was not deliberately, systematically wicked; and that as having been *deceived*, I am an object for commiseration, though not justified for *having deceived others*.

HISTORY OF THE FLAMALL FAMILY

You know but little more of my family and connexions, my dear Maclairn, than that I was the only daughter of a reputable attorney, who lived respected in modest affluence; and who died as he had lived, with an unblemished character. My mother, whose understanding and virtue would have done honour to any station in life, died when I was in my ninth year; and in her last illness she requested my father to place me, after her decease, in the house of the lady who had instructed her; and with whom she had continued to live on terms of intimacy and mutual regard. This lady's seminary had been gradually establishing itself in the opinion of the public, from the time that my mother had been one of its pupils; and it was at this period justly considered as one of the most respectable boarding-schools in London. Friendship for my mother, added to the governing principles of this excellent woman's mind, produced a tenderness for me, which was necessary in the first instance of my removal from my indulgent father; but I soon found that in my good governess I had a friend, and my school insensibly became my home. During this period of my life, I enjoyed every advantage which my fond father could supply; and his liberality extended to whatever was judged suitable for girls of large fortunes. It is necessary to mention Miss Flint's arrival, as a boarder, during my long residence in this house; but as I was two or three years younger than herself, I had formed my little *coterie*; and as I was not particularly attracted by her manners, we had no further intercourse, than such as resulted from being under the same roof. With the partiality of my father and my governess, I happily enjoyed peculiar marks of affection from my brother, who was some years my senior; and to him I stood indebted for my instruction in those branches of female accomplishments, which, as being very expensive from the attendance of capital masters, my father might have thought unnecessary for a girl in my station; but my brother judged of my talents so favourably, that no improvement could be useless to me. I had just gained my sixteenth year, when my dear father was suddenly removed, and my happiness interrupted. My governess kept me as a cherished guest till some days after the funeral, when she gave up her charge to an affectionate brother. It may not be improper to mention here an event which soon after deprived me of this inestimable friend. Easy on the side of fortune, and breaking in health, she gave up her school to another person, and retired to the west of England, where she had near relations. My grief for the loss of my father was for some time countenanced by the dejection of my brother Philip's spirits, and I discovered it to be my duty to restrain my tears before him. I even attempted the office of consoler, and assumed a cheerfulness with him which was remote from my feelings. One day I particularly endeavoured to lead him to a more resigned submission to the will of Heaven. He shook his head, and in a desponding tone, replied, "that he should not need my friendly admonition, could he forget his sister, but it was for *his Harriet* that he grieved." An explanation followed. My father's death had been accelerated by the difficulties which pressed upon him: he had just escaped being insolvent. Philip had incautiously, or rather with the honest pride of sparing to himself, and me, a disgrace so humiliating, administered; and the effects had been inadequate to the demands. He had consulted-his friends: had met with assistance and encouragement; and had every hope that diligence and economy would in time extricate him from his difficulties. In the mean time, I was his blessing; and if I could submit with cheerfulness to superintend his family for a season, he should be happy, and look forward to my more eligible situation. He now mentioned his connections, and the chances which were in his favour: hinting that my father had at least left him the integrity attached to his name, and a knowledge in his profession which none could dispute. I was not intimidated by this confidence, but I reminded him that my education had qualified me for a teacher: and that with Mrs. D—'s recommendation I had no doubt of being able to provide for myself. "We have one and the same interest," replied he, "to conceal our affairs from Mrs. D—, and from all the world. Whilst by my exertions I can keep matters as they now stand, I shall not be suspected of being a necessitous man. You know not the world you live in, my dear Harriet: we must keep up appearances, in order to surmount our difficulties. You are young and beautiful, and in time, may marry well. Till you can make a better exchange for my protection and love, than by degrading yourself, my last guinea shall be spent to support you. Have no fears, I will support my sister's claims to respect: you shall never serve for *wages*, till those of love fail." Penetrated by this goodness and generosity, it will be no matter of surprise to you, my dear Maclairn, that I trusted to this brother; and repaid his kindness by the most assiduous attention to his comforts and interest. For nearly a year I superintended his family with contentment; for Philip praised without ceasing his housekeeper, and frequently declared that he would not change me for the richest wife in the kingdom; for that I had established his credit by my management. I saw three clerks constantly employed in the office, my brother's regular attendance, and every appearance of business as in my father's time going on. The new year's day, I was told, that he was happy; for he could without inconvenience augment his dear Harriet's little allowance for clothes; that he wished to see me always dressed like Harriet Flamall, and the gentlewoman; though never like a girl on the look-out for a husband, or a simpleton ready to take up with any offer. I well understood that my brother was little disposed to favour what are called love-matches, at which his wit and ridicule were constantly pointed; but as I was neither exposed to those temptations, nor in any haste to change my condition, I received these indications of his prudence with gratitude; perfectly coinciding with him, that love was not the better for being houseless and unfed; and as I had no wealthy suitors, though some danglers, I was perfectly contented with being mistress of my brother's house, and seeing it his abode of peace. With youthful spirits and youthful vanity, I exulted in the regularity which presided at his table, and my heart was gay, when Philip said, "his Harriet was never taken by surprise, nor unfit to be seen." Kindness had given me an interest with his servants, which were two maids, and a foot-boy; and when my brother led a friend to his table, they good-naturedly forgot, that they had shared with their mistress the liver and bacon, or tripe, in order to sup on more costly viands. My brother's person and address were much in his favour, and it was not without some agreement on my part, that our acquaintance "wondered that the handsome and agreeable Mr. Flamall did not marry." Some hints given me by our chamber-maid, who, as I fancied, thought her master "too sober a gentleman," led me to suspect, that my brother had formed some connexion which stood in the way of a more honourable one; and whilst his regular visits into the country, in one certain direction, strengthened my suspicions, I could not help doing him justice for the consideration with which I was guarded from a knowledge of this supposed irregularity in his conduct; and sensible that his cautions in regard to mine were scrupulously exact and proper, I prudently left Philip to judge of the propriety of his own actions; and with unbounded trust believed, that if he erred, it was because he was human, and could not be altogether perfect, as I sometimes fondly thought him; whilst with the utmost solicitude he recommended to me the improvement of my time, and the prudence necessary for my security.

Under these happy circumstances of life, did I reach my seventeenth year, when towards the autumn, I was requested to prepare for the accommodation of a young man, who was to reside with us. Philip perceived my surprise. "It was not possible for me to avoid receiving him under my roof," added he; "his mother pressed the measure on me, with so much earnestness from her death-bed, that I had not the resolution to refuse her request; and standing as I do in the relation of a guardian to the young man, who has not a single connexion or friend in the world to whom he can turn, except myself, it is the more incumbent on me to provide for his safety. He is a modest lad; but at present a mere green-horn. He has been very ill since he has been in town, and I should not be surprised, if, with his excessive sorrow for the loss of his only friend, and the effects of his dreadful fever, he be plunged into a decline. You will be kind to him, my dear Harriet," continued he, "for you will pity him. If we can manage to get him well, he will become my pupil in the office, for he is poor, and must have some employment. He is sensible of this, and grateful for the education and little means which Mrs. Duncan has contrived to leave him."

A sick, consumptive, friendless youth, oppressed with sorrow for a mother's death, was a guest not to be placed in any inferior part of our house: my bed room was visited by the south sun, and had next to it, a light dressing closet, appropriated for my books and bureau. I was healthy; and the attic was equally convenient. The poor, dejected young man should find a home, and a neat retreat: and the books might help to divert his thoughts. This resolution was adopted. The following week, Mr. Charles Duncan made his appearance at our dining table; and on introducing him to me, Philip congratulated him with kindness on his improved good looks; whilst I, with emotions of pity, gazed on the finest youth my eyes ever beheld, blasted by sorrow and sickness. His deep mourning dress, the sober-sadness and dignity of his person, his collected demeanour and unstudied ease of manners, surprised me. From time to time, he spoke; his intelligent eyes were raised; and as the subject adverted to the recent events, his countenance marked the keenest sensibility, and the most profound grief. Without any of that aukward timidity, which I had been led to expect, he with politeness made his apologies for wishing to retire to his room, alledging that he had made exertions during the morning, which had fatigued him. Philip with much civility conducted him to his apartment. I had risen to receive his compliment on leaving the room, and felt a secret delight in reflecting, that he would find the one he sought suitable in those accommodations which he had a just title to expect under any roof. I still remained standing, lost in thoughts which perplexed me. The extreme caution of my brother in respect to me, seemed to have yielded to his zeal for a stranger; and I felt uneasy that I could not think Mr. Duncan a *lad just new to the world.* "But he is poor and friendless," thought I, "and my brother trusts to those disqualifications for my safety." A deep sigh followed; for I discovered, that poverty was no shield to my bosom. My brother's returning steps roused me from my reverie, and I sat down to the piano forte, to prevent my agitation from being noticed, and began to play a lesson which lay open on the music-desk, in the hope of evading any further conversation, relative to a guest, who I already discovered had gained too much of my attention. But Philip immediately reassuming the subject, and thanking me for giving up my room to the stranger, asked me what I thought of him. "Poor young man," replied I, "he looks consumptive and very melancholy. I should not be surprised if the air of London was found pernicious to health apparently so weak and declining." "He must take his chance on that point," answered my brother, "and should your prognostics be verified, I do not know whether I should regret his death. Under the circumstances of an illegitimate birth and friendless condition, life can afford but a very scanty portion for his hopes or enjoyments. It appears," continued my brother, "that Duncan, as he is called, is one of those unhappy beings, who are destined to share the iniquity of their mothers. His probably has worn the cloak of hypocrisy and concealment so long, that she has forgotten it was borrowed, or that she was the mother of a child whom she did not dare to acknowledge. I know that the good woman who has passed for his mother has left him a few hundred pounds, the savings from an annuity allowed her for this child's maintenance from his cradle." "But you know also his real mother," observed I with eagerness. "Indeed I do not," answered Philip, "nor does Duncan know her. I have some reasons for believing she lives in a foreign country; is a woman of birth and fortune; and probably one of those chaste dames, who thinks 'the world can never thrive,' &c. &c. I am sorry," continued my brother, "that I was not sooner known to Mrs. Duncan. I might have gained more insight into this poor young fellow's history, and perhaps his mother might have been induced to continue his annuity. But it was too late to press the business on a dying woman. She only declared, that she was not the real mother of Charles, commonly called Duncan; and requested he might be told so. I trusted to her papers for further information, but nothing satisfactory has appeared; and for the present, I think it is better to leave him to his regrets for the loss of his reputed mother, than to the bitter conviction of his birth and desertion." I entirely coincided in Philip's opinion; and our conference finished by my admiring his goodness and humanity, and vehemently reprobating the monster who could give up an infant to save herself from the reproach and shame she alone merited.

Mr. Duncan's health, for the space of more than a month, gave an ostensible colour to my attentions. I had pity, for the motive of an assiduity which, young as I was, my heart whispered was but the assumed name for love. My brother trusting, as I concluded, to the effects of his intelligence relative to his ward's fortune and disgraceful birth, for the security of a girl of seventeen, whose good sense and prudence were proverbial with him, left the interesting invalid to my unremitting cares, till the bloom of youth was restored, and Mr. Duncan was deemed in a condition to pass some hours in the office, in pursuance of his declared intention of studying the law. To what purpose should I detail the progress of a passion mutually excited under such circumstances as I have already mentioned? Let it suffice, that my lover was a stranger to the arts of seduction, and myself too inexperienced for the documents of worldly prudence, and too innocent for doubts or cautions.

Amongst the number of expedients we had ingeniously contrived, to elude my brother's knowledge of our union, till Mr. Duncan was of age, was one which appeared practicable and safe: my lover suggested it, and related to me the interest he had with the good woman under whose roof his mother had died. It appeared to him a providential interference, that had conducted them to Mrs. Keith's humane cares; for such was the name of the person with whom they lodged. "My dear mother," added Mr. Duncan, "was indebted to chance for the recommendation of lodgings in London, when she was a stranger. At Grantham we took up a lady apparently of some respectability in the neighbourhood of that town, for she was in a gentleman's carriage, when she inquired at the inn the hour at which the stage coach would reach London. She was a handsome, pleasant, and well bred woman, and good-humouredly communicative. My mother, in the course of our journey, expressed some regret on not having written to her only agent in town, to secure lodgings for her, observing that she did not much enjoy the thoughts of being forced to sleep in a common inn. The courteous stranger instantly engaged to conduct us herself to lodgings which she could recommend, adding, that her uncle, Counsellor Peachley, had recently quitted his apartments, for a country residence near town, and that by agreement, or rather favour, the Keiths had permission to let the rooms in his absence, for their own emolument. But this indulgence was, it appeared, limited; and the lady's good offices were requisite to our success. She kindly performed her promise, and I believe was farther useful to us in the distressing scenes which followed. My gratitude on leaving this house for your brother's, has, I believe, attached Keith and his wife to me. He serves the office of clerk in this parish church, and might assist us effectually. Your brother," added he smiling, "pays his devoirs regularly every Sunday in the country. You are tempted by a more popular preacher, to stray from Mr. G——'s flock, and I suspect that your servants are not scrupulous in the observance of their sabbath."

I complied with a project from which I had little to fear, well knowing that my brother's example had been contagious in his family. Our banns were published: Keith officiated as father at the altar, and his wife as my friend and companion, my appearance not contradicting hers. My husband demanded a certificate of our marriage, and I returned home with it in my bosom unsuspected.

With a circumspection rarely preserved in a union, where the sum total of years did not amount to forty, we eluded for a time all suspicion. My situation became the signal for terror and anxiety to break into that contentment of heart, which had succeeded to our marriage.

Duncan in vain urged the necessity of his openly declaring his claims to protect me. I opposed to his arguments my dependence on my brother, and his minority, which would for some months prevent his free agency. I pleaded the expected absence of Philip, who constantly left town in the summer vacation; and sanguinely brought forwards my project of preserving our secret by means of Mrs. Keith: thus passed the early months of my pregnancy. But I was unable to counterfeit health. My brother was alarmed by my cough; and my friends recommended to me country air. At this eventful period, *Mrs. Hatchway* with her daughter, now Mrs. Serge, paid their annual visit to London. Mr. Hatchway was master of a ship, and his wife and only child, Miss Lydia, contented with its accommodations, and fond of an element with which they were too familiar for fear, every summer made this little voyage; and stationing themselves in Wapping, enjoyed with unwearied activity the more remote and fashionable pleasures of the metropolis. They were our relations; and dining in Red-Lion square from time to time, during their short stay, had been the customary offering of good-will, and for which they liberally paid, by supplying us with turkies and red herrings in the winter. Their remembrances of this kind had been so abundant, that we on our side had enlarged our civilities; and Philip had for the two preceding visits, treated them with a sight of Sadler's Wells, or the Haymarket. On seeing my pale and emaciated form, they expressed much compassion; and, with the *utmost generosity*, they declared I should not be hurried to a crowd, in order to please them. My brother as warmly insisted that Miss Hatchway should not be disappointed of her amusement; and this contest finished by the good-natured mother's *heroically* saying, she preferred remaining with me. During the absence of the party, my ill-health was the subject of her conversation. Change of air and a voyage were urged: she was certain that sea air would restore me in a month. She remembered that her mother, before her marriage, was thought in a decline; and had been cured by residing a few months at Y——h. I immediately saw the advantages which might result from my quitting my brother's house;

but I had my husband to consult. This, however, I happily effected; for my restless cousin recollected a shop near us, in which she had purchased some article a few days before, and she wished for more of it. My cough again befriended me; it was near nine o'clock, and the evening unpleasant, so she sallied forth alone. My husband blessed heaven for this promised deliverance; he urged me to accept of the invitation, and declared that he would remove me from Y——h to Newcastle, and from thence to Leith: for that I should not return to my brother's, till my spirits were more equal to meet his resentment. At supper, the good captain seconded his lady. "He had long piloted his women." The cabin was neat; and I had nothing to fear in the "Charlotte." My brother counselled me to try the experiment; and my voyage was determined on. At the expiration of a few days the ship sailed. Our navigation was prosperous and delightfully pleasant. I was in no way incommoded; and the good friends with me, exulted on seeing me keenly devour sea-biscuit. Freed from the dread of my brother's inquisitorial eyes, and amused by the novelty of the scene, my spirits rose to cheerfulness; and I was led to consider my female friends with some curiosity and amusement. Mrs. Serge, at present, so strongly resembles her good mother in her person, that it is only necessary to observe that when young, she was extremely pretty. Nature had not been less faithful in the lineaments of their minds. Both enjoyed an exuberance of health and activity; a constant flow of animal spirits and good humour; to which was annexed an absence of thought or attention for the morrow. My observations soon led me, however, to doubt, whether their sum of positive happiness exceeded that of their fellow mortals. Their constant restlessness; their insatiable cravings for vanity and pleasure, might be fairly weighed with the cares of the ambitious, and the labours of the philosopher; and most assuredly were as fatiguing as the demands of vanity. A "frolic," to use Mrs. Hatchway's term for a jaunt of pleasure, was the supreme good in her opinion: it was necessary to her existence; and however qualified, all was a *"frolic"* which put her spirits in motion. Having been wet to the skin in an open cart; or slept in a barn on straw, or in a bed with half a dozen companions, only gave zest to the remembrance of the "fun" occasioned by any disaster. If the pleasure had smoothly rolled on in post-chaises, and a good dinner, and a good inn received them, their joy was complete; "for what was money made for, but to be spent? Those who *worked* had a right to *spend*." No grievance tormented them, but being stationary; nor did they believe there was a malady which a dance would not cure. To people of this description I could only plead the weakness of my bodily strength. We were safely landed at Y——h, the captain proceeding in his voyage to Sunderland. A neat habitation announced the opulence of my friends in that class to which they belonged. The first day was passed in settling ourselves, which was performed with admirable dispatch and order; for Mrs. Hatchway observed, that, "after a holiday, idleness was ingratitude." The next day was given to their neighbours, who were numerous; but I was indulged, and in my neat little chamber enjoyed the privilege of writing to my husband. At supper, my cousin told me, she had engaged me to see a ship launched. "We shall breakfast," added she, "with the captain's wife, who lives on the quay. As soon as the vessel floats, we shall go on board, and sail in her down the river. You will see also the fort and the pier; and in the evening we shall return home in *carts*; they are the fashion here, and the exercise they give, is strongly recommended to invalids." I had seen scores of these vehicles moving in the street, and instantly imagined that a *wheelbarrow*, although drawn by a horse, would not suit me. I pleaded fatigue, and without the smallest ill-humour appearing, I was told, that no welcome was worth a farthing, if folks were not left to judge for themselves: "so please yourself, my dear Harriet," added she, "and you will please me. I hope to see you, before you leave us, as eager to run after a fiddle, and as fond of a ride in a cart as this girl, who two years since was as fond of her own room as yourself; but I soon made her what you see her, as healthy a girl as any in England; and her aunt will tell you so, when she comes. I have no notion of patch-work, and darning muslin, which costs so dearly; Lydia was half killed by being with my sister. You will take care of yourself, my love," continued she; "Sarah will be left with you; and I can trust her."

She was not mistaken; Sarah was assiduous, and my tranquillity continued uninterrupted till one o'clock, when she informed me, that Mrs. Priscilla Hatchway, her master's sister, was in the parlour, and wished to see me. "There has been some blunder," added the girl; "for she is come to dine with my mistress." Civility compelled me to leave my retreat. A neat well-dressed woman of forty and upwards, rose to salute me, and with much good-nature congratulated me on my safe arrival. For some time I found my guest an intruder; but she insensibly engaged my attention, by talking of my mother, and flattered my self love, by observing, that I was her very picture. I learned that Mrs. Priscilla had fully expected to meet the family party. "I sent my sister word, yesterday," continued she smiling, "of my intention; but a ship-launch was too serious a business for me to interrupt, and they well know I am not apt to take offence where none is intended."

After dinner she proposed to me a walk; to this I had no objection; and she took the road to the fort. The level and fine turf I trod, with the prospect in view, beguiled the time: for on the left was the main ocean, and on the right the river, which, at the fort, forms the bar and the pier, useful for working the vessels from and into the harbour. We reached the ferry-boat which led to a village on the opposite side of the river; and we sat down. "I have had my designs in conducting you hither," said she; "that," pointing to a small neat habitation, "is my house; and you see how easy the road is which separates us. Have you any objections to our drinking tea there? I will conduct you home; and if the vagrants are returned, I will sup with them; for it is a full moon, and the boatman will wait my call." I acceded to this arrangement, and we soon reached the house, but with some surprise found the parlour filled with Mrs. Hatchway's friends, and she busily engaged in assisting the maid, to prepare a regale of fruit and tea. The good Mrs. Priscilla received with momentary gravity her sister's greetings and apology. This amounted, to having forgotten, in her hurry, to send her notice of her engagement, and intention of calling upon her in her way home. To this succeeded her pleasure of seeing me. "Nothing ever was more fortunate! for they expected a cart, and I might ride home." The company now claimed our attention. This consisted of several persons, but the principal care of Mrs. Hatchway was directed to a lady who had been "uncomfortable" on board the ship, being fearful of the water. I found she was from the country, and with her husband had a daughter of Miss Lydia's age. A survey of Mrs. Priscilla's parlour pleased me; it was furnished with good prints, and a handsome book-case; the windows commanded the sea, and a pretty garden hung from the elevated ground to the river. I expressed my approbation of her abode; and in the kindest manner she pressed me to try, what she called, *country* as well as *sea* air. I thanked her, and acknowledged that I thought her situation delightful. "Then sleep here to-night," answered she eagerly, "I will show you my little spare nest." I looked at Mrs. Hatchway. "Please yourself, and you will please me," said she with her usual good-humour. "Do, my dear Miss Flamall, consent to my aunt's proposal," cried Miss Lydia; "for then I shall see Beecles races." This settled the business. The strangers were accommodated with my room at Mrs. Hatchway's house, and my trunk was sent, for greater dispatch, that evening; and before my eyes were open the next morning, my Y——h friends were on the road to Beecles races. They called in their way at our door, and said their absence would not be for more than a *week*. On the maid-servant's delivering this message at our comfortable breakfast table, Mrs. Priscilla laughed, and said that her sister's *weeks* were not always regulated by the calendar: she had known some, that had extended to *six* of the common reckoning of time, "and should either a wedding, a christening, or a funeral intervene," added she, "you may find this *"frolic"* longer than you wish, unless you love quiet as well as I do." You will not be surprised that I wished for nothing but for letters from my Charles, and the prolongation of my friend's pleasures.

Duncan was made easy by my account of myself, and my new situation. I was happy in his assured love, and we mutually agreed to wait with patience till he could see me at G—ne. A fortnight had nearly elapsed; when, in the place of an expected letter from my husband, one arrived from Mrs. Hatchway. Fortune had been favourable. She was detained in spite of herself. Lydia was to be bride-maid to her young friend, and having had a letter from her husband, to inform her that he was going to Leith, she had indulged her friends in their request. Even this good news did not cheer me. I had missed receiving my cordial for two posts. The sympathizing Mrs. Priscilla dispatched a person the next morning to the Y——h post-office, and endeavoured to divert my attention till the woman's return. She brought me a letter: it had my brother's writing on the address. I turned pale, I suppose; for she smiled, observing that I might have another, and still more welcome letter on the morrow. "It is from my brother," answered I, still mournfully holding the fatal scroll in my hand. "Well, and you may have good news from *your brother*," replied she, rising. "So I will go and get you some strawberries, whilst you are busy."

Merciful heaven! From what unknown cause did it arise that I remained several minutes with this letter unopened in my hand! I recollected that I had not answered a former one; and that Philip hated writing letters. Some unknown terror seized my spirits; and I wept. At length I was mistress of its contents. "An *unpleasant*," (yes, that was the word,) "occurrence had engaged his time, and harassed his mind." *His ward, Duncan,* had absconded; a charge of a highway-robbery having been lodged against him at the Bow-street office. He had been summoned on the occasion to answer to some questions relative to the young offender; but he was sorry to say that his evidence in his favour could not set aside the proofs of his guilt. He had, however, acted prudently in withdrawing from the threatened prosecution. "I have done all in my power", added my brother, "to soften his accuser, but he is a determined man; and says that he cannot recede, in justice to the community, nor to himself." Much followed, in which my brother's vexation had for its object his own *reputation,* and the mortification of having it known that he had had connexions with a highway-robber.

I did not faint on reading this dreadful letter: no: I did not die, when death would have been a blessing! but grasping it with convulsive force, my whole frame shivering as in an ague fit, I remained motionless on my chair, conscious of the overwhelming tide of misery which was bursting on my head. At last impelled by ideas too dreadful to be recalled, and too vague to be ascertained, I hurried down stairs. The kitchen was my passage to the garden, and the fire, I believe attracted me; for I sat down by it, in a great-chair, which had its station in the chimney-corner, and bending over the hearth, my nerves relaxing; the horrid paper fell from my hand, and heedless of my danger, I gazed on the flame it raised. The maid-servant at this moment entered, and screaming out, that, "my gown would take fire," recalled me to recollection. I started, and with a deep drawn sigh, said "let me die!" When recalled to life, I found myself in my bed. My worthy friend was watching me: her looks bespoke distress and pity. "Be comforted," said she, "you are safe with me. Be composed, and trust to my care." Let it suffice, Harriet Flamall was saved from reproach and shame, and like thousands of her unhappy sex, was doomed to weep the loss of her infant, and to be thankful it lived not to partake of its mother's disgrace. Mrs. Priscilla Hatchway was, however, informed of my situation; and she advised me to give her my marriage certificate, which I had worn in my bosom. She enforced the prudence of my keeping my marriage a secret, till Mr. Duncan appeared. His letters to me had prepossessed her in his favour. "She did not believe he was capable of such an outrage as that of which he was accused." Every hour she repeated that it was impossible; and that it required with her more than presumptive proof to condemn any man, much more one whose sentiments were noble and pure.

I am prolix, my dear Maclairn: I will endeavour to be less so. Encouraged to hope, soothed to patience by this excellent woman, and, above all, led to think with her, that I should hear tidings of my husband from Mrs. Keith, I combated so effectually with my griefs, as to be able to suppress their appearance; and having seen my friends return to meet Captain Hatchway, I preferred, for several reasons, the conveyance of his cabin to any other. We had a tedious passage, which was highly beneficial to me; for on reaching my home, I was congratulated on my *good looks*. My brother was on an excursion; and I profited from his absence.

I went to Mrs. Keith's house. It was shut up; and *"to be lett."* Ready to sink, I entered the opposite shop, and made my inquiries. "Keith had been taken up on suspicion of forgery. No one could tell what was become of his wife. Their goods had been seized by the proprietor of the house, which was very hard, as the Counsellor who lived in the apartments in the winter months, had bought every thing for his own use; and had generously permitted them to let the rooms for their benefit six months in the year." Some comments were added to this account: "Mrs. Keith was pitied, and the shopkeeper finished by saying that it was a pity her husband had so long escaped justice, for he had been the ruin of many." A customer entered, and I quitted the shop with aggravated distress; for I could not avoid associating the guilt of Keith with my husband's fate.

Two days having passed under these impressions, had reduced my strength, and diminished my "good looks." My brother was shocked at my appearance, and listening only to my friends, he removed me to Kensington Gravel Pits, with a solicitude that wounded my feelings. More than once my secret was on my lips, but my resolution failed: I had no opportunity for disclosing the painful cause of my sufferings, and I hoped to die without wringing Philip's heart. My youth, in the mean time, resisted the attacks of sorrow: I recovered gradually; and sensible of the extraordinary expences which my brother had incurred in consequence of my illness, I urged him to give up the lodgings. He insisted on keeping them another month, adding, that the air was evidently salutary to me. I now heard Duncan named for the first time. My brother received a visit from an acquaintance, and pleading my inability to admit the visitor into the little parlour, they sat down on a garden-seat under the window, the sash of which was up, and I was screened by the blind. "Have you heard from that fool, Duncan?" asked the guest. My brother answered in the negative. "He was soon frightened, by what I can understand of his unlucky business," rejoined the stranger. "The fellow who appeared against him is too well known to be able to hurt any man. Every one believes Duncan perfectly innocent." "I wish I were one of that number," replied my brother; "but his going off, and never writing since, looks suspicious. We traced him to Harwich, and I have no doubt of his having crossed the sea. He cannot be insensible to the anxiety I must suffer on this occasion. I cannot pardon his ingratitude, for he was treated like a brother under my roof. However, when he can draw for his little fund, I shall see his name I do not doubt: in a few weeks more I shall hear that he has not forgotten the little money which he may without peril claim from me." The conversation then turned on the visitor's business, whom my brother attended a part of his way to town. I was forcibly struck by what I had heard. Duncan's cruel desertion of me; his apparent ingratitude to my brother; the society he had mixed in; his suspected crime, and neglect of writing, seized upon my heart. I resolved to conceal from my brother my connection with a reputed robber, and a man who had without pity left me to suffer the penalty of my weakness and credulity. My brother's peace was to be preserved; and I was firm to my purpose.

Again I remonstrated on the expence of the lodgings. "Say not a word on that subject, my dear Harriet, I intreat you," answered Philip. "In preserving you, I am preserving my own comforts. I would spend my last shilling to see you well and *happy*; but till you have more confidence in my affection, I must despair." "What is it you mean?" asked I in trembling doubt. "Not to alarm, not to distress you," replied he with solemnity. "Are you really well enough to return home? Are you equal to the exertions which your return to society will demand? Can you be cheerful, and prepared for every accident? Answer these questions. I mean not to reproach; but *to heal*. I will not," continued he, taking my cold hand, "leave you in suspense. I am no stranger to your fatal engagements with an unprincipled man. Nothing of this indiscretion can be recalled; but in a discovery of *your marriage* is involved *my ruin* as well as your own. When you are more composed, I will be more explicit; in the mean time rely on my prudence and love. Weak and errring as your conduct has been, I will yet trust to your reason and principles. Let these resolve the question. Are your peace and happiness, my success and reputation in life, to be sacrificed to a romantic attachment to a *villain*, whose name is already a reproach to us, merely because we sheltered him?" He quitted me much agitated, and unable to witness my agony.

My brother's lenity was not lost upon me. Grateful for his forbearance, touched by his arguments, I assiduously endeavoured to appear what he wished. My occupations were renewed; and my serenity was such, as imposed on my acquaintance. The poor and wretched wanderer was regarded, as one whom it was my duty never to name, never to believe otherwise than guilty of the crime laid to his charge, nor ever to be acquitted of having abandoned me. Sometimes I recalled to memory his conversations relative to his early life, and the suspicions he entertained of his not being Mrs. Duncan's son. Among the reasons he assigned for this opinion, was her anxiety to see him *accomplished*, as well as solidly instructed; her never proposing any plans for his future provision, and the silence she preserved in respect to his resources, and her own. I once mentioned to Mr. Duncan my brother's account of Mrs. Duncan's declaration. He was apparently agitated; and I regretted my too fond loquacity; whilst he endeavoured to console me for my indiscretion. In the variety of my painful reflections, I sometimes conjectured that Mr. Duncan had discovered his parents; and finding his rank and expectations incompatible with his engagements with me, had withdrawn from the kingdom: that he had even concerted the story which had been circulated; and trusting to a splendid name and fortune for favour with the world, had left the name of Duncan to reproach and infamy; and his wretched wife to sink into the grave. These ideas prevailed for a season; and were then discarded with disdain, as unworthy of him and myself. Tenderness, trust, and his fond and unambitious heart had their turns. Thus fluctuating, I determined to speak to my brother; he had said, that he would be more *explicit* with me, when I was in a state to be treated with entire confidence; and I reminded him of his promise, adding at the same time that I found the doubts which distracted my mind unfriendly to every purpose of my reason, and too much for my religious faith; I could not be resigned, till I was convinced that I should see my husband no more.

"I have expected the application," answered he, with calmness, "and I am prepared for it. It is not amiss that you should be informed of all that is known of this unhappy man. Notwithstanding our friends carefully avoid a subject, which they well know has given me more vexation than any occurrence of my life, something may accidentally drop which will affect you. I have seen that my Harriet has fortitude, and when you are acquainted with the circumstances which have convinced me of this wretched man's guilt, you will the more steadily pursue that line of conduct which becomes you. I will leave you a few minutes to yourself," added he, unlocking his scrutoire, and taking from it a letter, which he gave me. "Only promise me, that you will not lose sight of your Philip, in your sorrow for a worthless husband." He pressed my hand to his bosom, and left the room. The letter before me was addressed to Mr. Flamall, in the well-known characters of my husband. I was still weeping over it, when Philip returned, and without speaking, placed himself opposite to me with visible anxiety. The contents of the letter were as follow.

LETTER LIII

From Charles Duncan to Mr. Flamall.

"Sir,

"You will see me no more. My mysterious conduct will be soon fatally explained to you. Let it suffice here, that I avow myself the husband of your sister, and that the purpose of my soul was to have seen, once more, my beloved, ruined wife. But I was not equal to the task of telling her, that she must forget *Charles Duncan*. Let her not curse him, gracious heaven! although he is culpable, *even guilty!* Lost to honour and to happiness, still will he pray for her, and die her faithful, though wretched

"Duncan."

"P. S. The twenty guineas you advanced for my journey have been the means of preserving my miserable existence. You shall hear from me again when I am more collected, and in a situation less critical. I implore from you a regard and tenderness for your sister. May the Almighty fill your heart with compassion for her!"

Philip suffered my agony to be relieved by a flood of tears, without interruption, but not without sympathy. He was visibly moved by my condition. At length, taking my hand, he said; "I do not know, my dear Harriet, whether I am acting right by thus indulging your wishes at the hazard of distressing you; but if I could hope this painful remedy might, in the end, prove efficacious, by convincing your understanding and your principles of the folly, as well as the sin, of ruining your health by regrets which you ought not to indulge for so worthless an object, I would willingly satisfy your curiosity by detailing every circumstance of this unhappy affair: being persuaded that you will no longer judge me too severe in my opinion of this young man, nor scruple to think yourself bound to believe that he ought no longer to engage your thoughts, or to have a place in your heart." "Proceed," said I, "let me be convinced that there is not on earth a hope for me!" "This language is that of a girl," replied he gravely, "my sister will be taught by experience to think it so, and the time, I trust, is not remote, when she will bless heaven for the desertion of a man whom she now deplores, and she will consider his *flight* as a blessing, when contrasted with all the consequences which would and must have followed his remaining in this country."

"Long before your excursion to Y――h," continued my brother, "I suspected Duncan's conduct, and also somewhat of your unhappy partiality in his favour. I consequently observed *him* more narrowly, not *you*, my Harriet; for I, with all your friends, believed you too circumspect and prudent, to be in danger from a a young man in Charles's situation of life, however your fancy might have been allured to like his person. I was not satisfied with his pursuits, nor his connections; and, above all, with his reserve in respect to these. I was told that he gambled; and that, not with the inconsideration of heedless youth, but with the cool intrepidity of a veteran at the gaming-table; but I could never discover his haunts. More than once I saw his purse more amply furnished with gold than I could account for, yet my intelligencer had remarked that he had been of late an unsuccessful player, and I began to believe from his change of conduct about this period, that he had, like most unguarded young men, been drawn in to play by a little good fortune, and then dismissed to his sad experience for want of more money to lose. He was out of spirits, rarely from home, and diligent in the office. I resolved, therefore, to leave him to his own reflections, and the good fruits of repentance for the errors into which he had been betrayed. Soon after you left town, I happened to be with him in the clerks' office when a person called upon me for the payment of a small bill. A deficiency of silver led me to ask him to lend me a few shillings; he did so; and again I was surprised at seeing many guineas in his possession. The man had no sooner quitted us, than I observed to him, that finding his purse so well lined, I should not reproach myself for want of punctuality in the payment of his quarterly supply, nor wonder at his not having reminded me that it had been due a fortnight." He coloured; and I added, "One would think Duncan, you had either stumbled on a concealed treasure, or found one in your concealed parents." "I am not a spendthrift," replied he haughtily, "and I know I have at least one parent who will never abandon me, and whose resources are infinite." We were interrupted. Two or three days passed: I was reserved, and he sulky; when he surprised me, by asking my permission to be absent for a week or ten days. I hesitated. "Am I not to be informed whither, and with whom you are going?" asked I coldly. He replied, that he was going to Harwich, where he hoped to hear of those to whom in future he should be responsible for his actions: that, in the mean time, he should receive as a favour and indulgence from me, the permission he had requested. My clerk, Simons, good-naturedly remarked, that Charles had fagged hard during the absence of the other clerk, and he had a right to a jaunt: it would do him service; for he did not look well. Impressed by an idea, that he had heard something of his relations, I gave my consent to an absence of ten days; and at the same time paid him his quarter's arrears of twenty pounds. He promised to write to me from Harwich; and I left the office to join my friends who had engaged me in a party to Windsor. Two days elapsed before I returned home. I was prepared to find Charles absent: and, whilst at the dining-table, I asked casually, at what time Mr. Duncan had set out on his journey. The servant replied, that he had left the house the same evening with myself. Mr. Simons had supped with him at the inn, and had seen him mount his horse before he left him. "I hope he did not see him tipsy too," answered I, smiling; "but by the hour, I should fear that neither the one nor the other was fit for a journey, either on foot or on horseback." The servant said, that Mr. Duncan did not wait for the morning, it being his intention to ride a stage by moon light. "And how did he manage for his clothes?" asked I. "His trunk was sent by the coach on Monday," replied the lad. "There was something in this account which I did not like; particularly his removing his things, before he knew I should consent to his leaving the house. I expressed my surprise to Simons, who said he was in that plot, for he well knew that I should not be able to refuse the poor fellow, and he had set his heart upon going on horseback; so I advised him," continued he, "to send his portmanteau by the stage at all hazards, and when he had your leave, I carried him to a livery stable to look at a horse which I thought would suit him. It was a fine animal; and the youngster was so well pleased with him, that he hired him of my friend for the journey; and, young man like, said, he would ride him to Rumford before he slept: so we adjourned to a chop-house, where I supped with him, and at ten o'clock I saw him off; although the moon cheated him, for it was raining hard, and I thought he was a fool to seek a wet coat instead of a good bed." I had perceived in Simons something of that cunning, or to speak more plainly, knavery, which for many months had rendered me uneasy. He was a useful man, however, in the office, and I still employed him. I now thought there appeared a secret intelligence between him and Duncan; I dissembled, notwithstanding, and dropping the subject, applied to the business before me. A man shortly after brought a letter to Simons. It was from Duncan, and the purport of it was, I found, to inform him, that finding the horse unfit for the journey, he had sent him back, requesting him to settle the business with his friend, and to tell him that he had narrowly escaped a broken leg by trusting to his judgment. Simons swore, according to custom, and followed the messenger. I was told that he had paid for the horse's journey to Rumford, and that Duncan would remember travelling in the dark for some time, having been thrown from a horse too good for him. Judge of my astonishment on receiving a summons on the following morning to appear before the sitting justices. I found it was to be examined relatively to my *clerk, Charles Duncan,* and to meet a person in the office, who had positively sworn to his having been stopped on the Rumford road by Charles Duncan, and robbed of his watch and purse.

I listened with horror to the reading of this gentleman's deposition. It was clear and positive in every point that ascertained the criminality of the action, and the identity of the horse which Duncan rode. A crape concealed Duncan's face, and the accuser observed that he appeared to be a "young adventurer." Some appearance of lenity in the manners of the gentleman, who was a man in years, induced me to relate as much of Duncan's story as had come to my knowledge; but I pleaded in vain: a warrant was issued for apprehending him. You may judge, my dear Harriet, of the state of my mind when, on returning home, instead of finding Simons in the office, to whom I was anxious to give the particulars I have related to you, I found a letter from him on his desk, addressed to myself. It was couched in an insolent style. "He had not time to settle accounts with me, but thought his long and faithful services entitled to the consideration of using, for a very special and pressing occasion, the trifle of cash he had in his hands on my account." This was about five-and-twenty pounds. He warns me to try my influence with Duncan's prosecutor, as matters carried to extremity against my sister's husband, would not tend to my credit. "Shall I proceed?" added Philip with emotion; "need I describe my sensations! Your marriage, and the wretches with whom you had confederated to blast my happiness and reputation, for a time overcame me. But my sister soon resumed her wonted power in my soul. Providence appears to have seconded my fond hope of rescuing you from the snares that encompassed you. Your youth and credulity here found a compassionating friend, infinitely more able than myself to befriend you. We may rest in the full conviction of never being molested by Duncan or Simons. Keith has finished his career in a gaol, to which a suspicion of aiding in a forgery conducted him. His death was occasioned by a wound in his head, in consequence of his attempt to escape justice, and his wretched wife is at this time a nurse at the Lock-Hospital, for which post she is qualified.

"Such are the people, and such the lover to whom you gave up your fame and prospects in the world! Be grateful to heaven, my dear girl, for a deliverance from such connections so little to be expected, and give me the only recompense I ask for the hours of anxiety you have caused me. Let me see you under my roof, and with my name sustain the character which becomes Harriet Flamall, and promise me never to acknowledge your worthless husband."

Oppressed by my brother's kindness, and confounded by his relation of *facts*, as I conceived, in which Duncan was so dreadfully implicated, I eagerly engaged to preserve, for his sake, the fatal secret of my marriage, and to live for his comfort and service. He was satisfied, and left me to compose my spirits.

From this time it seemed to be tacitly agreed between us, not to name Charles Duncan, and I exerted my spirits now to a cheerfulness, which, although assumed, contented my brother; but, alas! what had I gained! The art of concealment, and the secret of hoarding up my sorrows for my private hours! My faded form was still attractive, and my brother one day complimented me on having, by *"sweet pensiveness and winning modesty,"* captivated a lover worth my notice, mentioning at the same time the gentleman's large fortune, independence, and hopes of gaining my favour. I with firmness assured my brother, that, in relinquishing the name and character of a married woman, it was my intention to have ever before me the vows I had plighted in the face of my Maker, and that as Mr. Duncan's wife I would live and die. He endeavoured to reason me out of this "scrupulous folly," as he called it. "Urge me not," replied I, bursting into tears, "lest I offend you by saying more. I would forego pomp and riches, this world's favour, and the accommodations necessary to my existence, for the chance of seeing him what he once was. I would traverse the globe with him; I would share in his misery, and partake in his toils without a murmur, could I find him. With these sentiments to support me in my duty, I shall at once say to any man who importunes me with offers of marriage, that I am *Charles Duncan's wife.*" My brother was displeased. He called me an "infatuated woman, a romantic fool," with other epithets, which I shall omit. I did not resent this harshness, and a year passed without the subject of a lover being named, or any appearing to put my constancy to the test. At this period I was surprised by seeing Philip enter the little closet in which I usually passed my vacant time. My Charles had augmented its attractions by decorating it with his drawings, and enlarging the number of the books. I instantly perceived that my brother had an impressive manner. He sat down beside me, tenderly chid me for my preference of this closet, and added, that he was afraid I should want fortitude to meet the intelligence he came to communicate in a spot so devoted to the purpose of nourishing unavailing grief. I trembled, and would have spoke—But— —